MW01147533

Praise for Scott Bradfield

"The most original voice of the new generation of Californian writers." *Brian Moore*

"Painfully beautiful writing." *Mary Gaitskill*

"Bradfield is one of my favorite living writers." *Jonathan Lethem*

"A wizardly writer of stories. His prose is so lucid and exact, his narrative sense so confident, that you hardly know where he's taking you until you're there." *Tobias Wolff*

"Scott Bradfield has been writing some of the wisest and funniest fiction for a while now." *Sam Lipsyte*

"A howlingly funny, too-neglected American writer!" *The Believer.*

"Scott Bradfield has not simply staked out new literary terrain… he has mapped and colonized an entire new planet." *Michael Chabon*

"A writer with a gift for characterization, as well as a delightfully wild imagination." *Stephen Amidon*

Books by Scott Bradfield:

Fiction:

The History of Luminous Motion (1989)
Dream of the Wolf: Stories (1990)
What's Wrong with America (1994)
Animal Planet (1995)
Greetings From Earth: New and Collected Stories (1996)
Good Girl Wants it Bad (2004)
Hot Animal Love: Tales of Modern Romance (2005)
The People Who Watched Her Pass By (2010)
Dazzle Resplendent: Adventures of a Misanthropic Dog (2017)

Criticism:

Dreaming Revolution (1993)
Confessions of an Unrepentant Short Story Writer (2012)
Why I Hate Toni Morrison's Beloved: *Several Decades
of Reading Unwisely* (2013)

Dazzle
Resplendent

adventures of
a misanthropic dog

SCOTT BRADFIELD

London: Red Rabbit Books, 2017

DEDICATION

For Bernie Sanders, Ralph Nader, Noam Chomsky, Democracy Spring, Brand New Congress, and the best of their species.

CONTENTS

Acknowledgments

Our understanding of ourselves goes from bad to worse!

–Nietzsche

ACKNOWLEDGMENTS

These stories originally appeared in *Other Edens 2*, *The Magazine of Fantasy & Science Fiction*, *Fence*, *Neue Rundschauer*, and *The Baffler*.

1. DAZZLE

DAZZLE WAS A dog with bushy red hair, fleas and an extraordinary attention span–especially for a dog. He was particularly fond of pastry, philosophies of language and Third World political theory. It was Dazzle's express opinion that unless somebody started paying the Third World a little concerted attention, serious consequences faced all mankind. Philosophies of language, on the other hand, were just a hobby, and when it came to pastry Dazzle preferred Sarah Lee Strawberry Cheesecake. There was more dog than dogness about Dazzle. Generally Dazzle knew how to keep his mouth shut, and strenuously avoided calling any attention to himself.

"The little doggy go woof," said Jennifer Davenport, the youngest member of Dazzle's patron family, the Davenports. Jennifer was six years old. Whenever anybody visited they said how beautiful Jennifer was. Dazzle thought Jennifer was just okay. "Woof, doggy. Be a good goddy–oops, I said doog goddy, I mean–" Jennifer looked theatrically around at her family, who had positioned themselves

3

conscientiously around the living room television, but nobody looked back.

Doggies don't go woof, Dazzle thought, suffering Jennifer's cold hand on his nose. The *Canis familiaris* utters a guttural dipthong, much like the Mandarin Chinese dipthong, only less enunciated. Now why don't you leave me alone and go watch a little TV. Jennifer was already tempted. The television radiated warm noise and a flickering colorless haze that illuminated the faces of Father, Mother, Billy and Brad like nuclear isotopes. Mother was the Big One who fed Dazzle. Billy was the Little One who took him for the best walks.

DOGS DON'T LIKE people, Dazzle thought. Dogs like dogs. Dazzle liked Homer, a resolute and well-groomed Dalmatian who often roamed the park during Dazzle's afternoon walks, and Dingus, the hideous Lhasa Apso who snorted at Dazzle through the slatted pine fence of Dazzle's backyard. "Life's a game, Dingus," Dazzle would say, contentedly pawing his rawhide bone and gazing up at the blue, translucent sky.

"Life's a game, and you learn to play it by the rules, or else you learn to make everybody else play by *your* rules. You can either be the ruler or the ruled, and that's the crux, isn't it, old pal? That's the decision we've all got to make. Me, I'd rather live by the rules I'm dealt. I'm no high achiever, Dingus. I like my life. I eat well and get plenty of exercise, and I've pretty much got this whole yard to myself most days. Of course, I'm what you'd have to call an exceptional dog, but being exceptional's one of those things that takes a lot of effort, let me tell you. Being exceptional takes lots of hard work, work, work. Being exceptional just means lots of pain and suffering. Look at Kerouac. Look at Martin Luther King. They were exceptional, and where'd being exceptional get *them*? I'll tell you where it got them. It got them nowhere at all.

Dingus snuffled against the pine fence. "Dog smells," he said. "Food and water and dog smells." Dingus snorted and snuffled and eventually lay down in the warm dirt and fell asleep. In his dreams of quick rabbits, Dingus kicked. "Rabbits," he muttered in his sleep. "Quick rabbits."

Some days, though, Dazzle was so depressed he couldn't get out of bed to go to the bathroom. He lay on his desultory, twisted blanket beside the water heater in the basement and awaited the occasional click of the thermostat and the rush of the gas fire that indicated Mother was washing dishes or doing laundry. Dazzle never knew what it was exactly. He just felt a vague, indefinable anxiety, a fundamental sadness at the inconclusiveness of things. It was the way he felt when he saw a dead cat in the road. Dazzle hated cats, but when he saw them squashed and senseless in the spattered street he didn't hate them anymore. He sniffed at them; they didn't even smell like cat. They smelled like hot asphalt, transmission fluid and gasoline. Sometimes Dazzle just lay on his blanket for hours, contemplating the meaninglessness of dead cats. When the postman pushed mail through the grate he might try to emit a halfhearted growl, but usually he didn't bother. Eventually he would hear Billy's bike clattering onto the dirt driveway, and force himself shaggily to his feet, shaking off his loose, dandruffy hairs. Dazzle simply didn't have any clear idea what was bothering him, but did his best to maintain a good false front. He didn't want people to think he was just feeling sorry for himself.

"It's a good life," he told Homer in the park. Billy was sitting on the softball bleachers with his friends and absently handling Dazzle's disenfranchised leash. "Of course, it's a routine, we all know that. A dog's life, as they say. Dog days in a dog's life and all that. But you take away routine and what have you got? Have you read the papers lately? Do you know what the world population figures are going into the next century? Check it out, pal; check it out. And do you know what our President's official policy is on overpopulation? Well, hold still just a second and I'll tell you. Our President thinks any increase in population only creates a larger, wealthier consumer market. That's what our President thinks. The more overpopulated the world gets, the more Volvos we sell. The more canned spinach. The more Levi's. The world's going to hell in a handcar, Homer, let me tell you. So routine, well, maybe it's a bit boring. But it's better than no routine at all–and you know what no routine at all means, don't you, Homer? It means chaos, entropy, deindividuation, madness and death. How's that sound to you, Homer? Does that sound better than one square meal a day, and a warm blanket to sleep on? Does it, Homer? Because maybe, just maybe, *I've* had it wrong all these years."

"Relax and eat a bone," Homer said, imperiously panting, gazing off dreamily at a big black bird on a wire. "Gnaw a bone and dig the yard." Homer was a sage and sensible dog, Dazzle thought. But he was also, like every other dog Dazzle had ever met in his entire life, extraordinarily stupid. Even Dazzle's brave and obvious exercises in false bravado were lost on stupid dogs like Homer and Dingus.

It was a very lonely world, Dazzle thought. This world of dogs.

NIGHTS DAZZLE SUFFERED long knotty bouts of insomnia which arose in him as charged, eccentric monologues filled with delusions of grandeur and then, just as impossibly, plunged him into the depths of irony, self-mockery and suicidal despair. "The best lives are simple lives," Dazzle tried to convince himself, unable to sit still for a minute. He heard the mice in the garbage, the beetles in the walls. He got up and turned and turned again on his frazzled blanket. Then, of course, the irrepressible antitheses arose too. "Simple lives are filled with loneliness, vacancy and self-deception." For days he would go without eating, just gazing emptily at the liquefying Gravy Train in his big plastic red bowl. Flies settled in it; then, at night, the mice came. It didn't really matter, he thought. Sometimes, when he urinated on the newspapers, a few tiny drops of blood dripped out. His stomach twitched and growled; he experienced long energetic periods of flatulence. Some days he couldn't even bear the thought of facing the world's other dogs.

The family veterinarian, Hsiang the Merciless, prescribed antibiotics. This is life's real horror, Dazzle thought, prone on the ice-cold metal table, closing his eyes and abiding the flea spray's aerosol hiss. Streams of black fleas spilled across the thin tissue sanitary sheet. We live and we die by the thousands, Dazzle thought. And in order to live, we visit our doctor. Dr.

Hsiang's gloved hands prodded and violated Dazzle in every conceivable way, and in many inconceivable ones. Dazzle shivered with terror, surrounded by the cold, antiseptic office, the menacing banks of glittering stainless-steel blades and instruments. This is the horror of life, he thought. This is life's trial, and then we die.

When Billy hid the antibiotic pills in tiny edible lumps of Dazzle's Alpo, Dazzle would carefully disengage and deposit them behind the hot water boiler where nobody, to his knowledge, ever cleaned. He had heard too much about the debilitating effect of antibiotics on the body's immune system, and anyway, he knew his grief was not physiochemical. It was philosophical, ethical and spiritual. It was a logical problem he had to deal with. Intellectually, he knew he was on firm ground. Maybe life wasn't filled with all the excitement and challenge he might have desired, but, he reflected, you can't always change life. You can't always change history, Kenneth Burke once said, but you can change your attitude toward history. Dazzle had a bad attitude, for which he could only hold himself responsible. Fundamentally, Dazzle considered himself an existential humanist. This meant he didn't believe in God, but he did believe in guilt.

"Good dog. Nice dog. Dazzle is a nice dog," the psychiatrist said, cradling Dazzle's freshly laundered blanket in his arms as if it were a baby. The psychiatrist was balding and slightly pockmarked; he wore thick wire-rimmed glasses. "He looked a little ludicrous, if you want to know the truth," Dazzle told Dingus later. The psychiatrist's name was Dr. Bernstein, and Dr. Bernstein told Mr. Davenport that

Dazzle suffered from acute feelings of insecurity initiated by a birth trauma and castration. ("I think it was castration," Dazzle said. "You want to talk about trauma, let's forget birth altogether. Let's talk about getting your balls chopped off. Bastards." Dingus snuffled miserably.) "Nice dog. Good dog," Dr. Bernstein continued, burying his silly face in the blanket and sniffing audibly at it as if he, and not Dazzle, were the dog. Then he smiled. "Dazzle smells nice. Dazzle's blanket smells nice." Once each week Dazzle lay on the tiny hearth rug beside the electric fire, peering up at the visibly disturbed and often unsettling Dr. Bernstein. Dr. Bernstein pranced about, emitted barking and growling noises and offered Dazzle a red rubber chew toy which Dazzle contemplated lying before him like a mantra or something by Wittgenstein. "I think it's true what they say about psychiatrists," Dazzle said later. "They're all crazy as fruit bats." As Dazzle said this, Dingus lay down in the dirt and began licking himself noisily.

Veterinarians, canine shrinks, other dogs, Big and Little Ones. Things seemed to be getting worse and worse rather than better and better, at least so far as Dazzle's state of mind was concerned. The Family even began to regard Dazzle with a sort of diffracted familiarity. "Hi, Dazzle," they said, without bending to pet him. "How you doing, boy?" They looked genuinely concerned, but they also looked like they didn't want to get too involved. Dazzle didn't know what to say. Every evening he watched them assemble around the glowing television and sometimes, out of the corners of their eyes, they watched him watching them. He sat and listened unemotionally to the news.

The entire world was rapidly being transformed into a gigantic petrochemical dump, Dazzle thought. We are all being steadily infiltrated by carcinogens, toxins, radiation and some sort of irrepressible sadness that is probably the only underlying meaning anyway. Jennifer never snuck Dazzle into her room anymore so he could sleep on her bed. By now, though, Dazzle had learned to prefer the garage.

THEN ONE COLD afternoon, while Dazzle was in the backyard talking to Dingus, he noticed the gate was open. The latch had not engaged; and the wind was beating it gently against its creaking hinges. Dingus noticed it first, and began snuffling and darting back and forth against his own fence, insensibly sensing the sudden miracle of Dazzle's. "Cats!" Dingus cried. "Piss everywhere! Kill all the cats!" Dazzle watched his frenetic neighbor with a cool and cynical distemper. The bravest dogs are the dogs who bark behind fences, Dazzle thought wearily, got up and went to the gate which, with a tiny pull from his paw, swung widely open to reveal the rolling hills of the Simon Hills Estates covered with uniform tract houses. With a sinking feeling in his chest, Dazzle stepped outside into the unfenced world.

For days and days he wandered aimlessly, urinating weakly on trees, lampposts and hydrants with a distracted, almost surreptitious expression, as if he were secretly determined to eliminate all the world's traces of other dogs. His legs carried him steadily and rhythmically in no direction at all, and for a while he preferred this primal, nomadic state of consciousness. "It's not the rhythm of the primitive we've lost," Dazzle said out loud sadly, to nobody in particular.

"It's the rhythm of history itself." Other dogs often appeared and sniffed at Dazzle, and with impatient formality, Dazzle sniffed back. "Don't eat our food or piss on our posts," the dogs said. "Don't fuck our bitches." Dazzle disregarded the blind caution of their first warning, contemplated the ironic sadness of their second. One night, while he tried to sleep in an alley, he was approached by a bitch in heat. She was filthy and bone-hungry, and stank terribly. He looked up drowsily as she sniffed at him. "Sorry, dear," he said, watching her lumber off in her manic, erotic daze. We just bang around the world like that, Dazzle thought. We travel around the world banging into things.

Out here in the unfenced world, Dazzle's dream life gathered strange energy and momentum. They were muted, vegetable dreams, filled with formless bodies and soundless words, and when Dazzle awoke he found himself inexplicably contemplating the migration of birds, the constellations of his youth. He remembered as a pup lying out on the backyard's green grass with his chew toys and identifying them: Orion, Taurus, Hydra, the Pleiades. His sharp canine eyes could discern the rings of Saturn, the moons of Jupiter. Space was filled with awesome distances and complications. It went on forever and ever. Quasars, pulsars, stars, galaxies, vast convoluted nebulas like memories, shattered planets and exploding stars. As Dazzle grew older all this universal wonder seemed to shrink and encapsulate him like a glove. He forgot his own wonderment, or considered it frivolous. "I'm no adventurer," he used to tell the equally youthful Dingus. "I'm a house pet. I know how to keep my four paws planted right here on old terra firma." Recalling now his heartless and cynical affectations,

Dazzle started to cry. He didn't understand this inexpressible sadness, and wished it would end and leave him in peace. He wanted to be happy in his yard again. He wanted his bland regular meals and his blanket. He wanted that hard, musty world in which he knew the locations of things. He desired the simple dreams before language began, and regretted his own smug complicity in the world's systematic disavowal of imagination.

Needless to say, however, Dazzle didn't find much imagination out in the unfenced world either. Instead he found rampant street crime, bulleting cars and buses, underfunded public transportation, political corruption, sad songs, homeless families, bad meat and tall office buildings. "Sometimes there's just nothing you can say," Dazzle told himself, chewing morosely at a slice of stale bread he had pilfered from some addled pigeons. "Sometimes there aren't any explanations. Or if there are explanations, they don't make you feel any better." He slept in parks, alleyways, underneath parked automobiles, sensing his own true home diminishing in the world and reeling further and further away, like stars and nebulas and other planets in a universe of constant motion. All the stars in the world are hurtling further apart, Dazzle thought. Dissolution, heterogeneity and death. Even the Davenports were fading from the map of Dazzle's mind. Soon, Dazzle thought, the map will only contain direction and gravity and heat. It will lack a central landmark. There will just be the world, and me in it. It was hard for Dazzle to believe he could feel any more forlorn and helpless than he had when he was living with the Davenports, but now his sadness was actually inarticulable. He couldn't even compose sentences about how he felt; he couldn't alleviate the weight of his misery with metaphors or figurative language of any sort. His monotonous legs carried him deeper into the world of noise and lights and cities. Sometimes he encountered stray coyotes, or wild wolves who had gotten lost for years in the big cities and were now almost completely insane. They talked out loud to themselves and yelped pitifully at the least sudden sounds. They suffered from skin diseases, vitamin deficiencies and a wild, unexaggerated fear of all mankind. Howl at the moon, Dazzle told them. The moon is a bitch.

DAZZLE WAS SLEEPING in an overturned trash can on a neglected and undeveloped Encino lot when he met Edwina. Edwina was a nice dog, though excessively lean, who suffered from chronic indigestion and a severe overdependency on father figures. "Feed me," she said. "Beat me. Hurt me. Love me." She bowed her head as she approached Dazzle's trash can, sniffing suspiciously at Dazzle's unalpha-like yawn. "Sit down and rest," Dazzle said, shifting to one side. Edwina sniffed more intimately. "Forget it," Dazzle said. "Go to sleep," and Edwina did. This was the closest Dazzle had ever come in his life to a real relationship, and as such he blithely accepted much which, intellectually, he considered impossible or irrational. For while most of the time Edwina was disturbingly submissive, at other times, entirely without warning or apparent provocation, she would take vicious and sudden bites out of Dazzle's rump or tail. "Jesus Christ!" Dazzle would say. Edwina was like a beheaded or defaced street sign. There was very little understanding Edwina, which actually reassured Dazzle in a strange way, for Dazzle was a dog who for many years had felt he could understand just about anything, particularly dumb dogs.

Edwina didn't know anything, and relied on Dazzle to find food, evade dog catchers and traffic and some nights even to get to sleep. "Everything's going to be okay," Dazzle comforted her, gazing out at the starless, smoggy sky. "You just relax and leave everything to me." Edwina was a hopeless case and even more screwed-up than Dazzle, and that was why Dazzle suspected, at times, that he just might love her. "You aren't actually going to eat that, are you?" he might ask, or "Try taking a little bath in the pond in the park. You'll feel better." Whenever Edwina was in heat, she would bring home the mangiest, smelliest and most disreputable dogs she could find and fuck them in the bushes behind Dazzle's trash can. Afterward the spent and irritable dogs would try to pick fights with Dazzle, or bully him into giving away some of the food he kept wrapped up in newspapers inside his trash can. "One of these days, Edwina, you're going to get fucked by the wrong sort of character," Dazzle warned her after a very long night. "You know what that means, don't you? Rabies. Yeah, you heard me. Frothing at the mouth. These enormous lesions develop along your spine and inside your brain. You'll be one crazy bitch, Edwina. I mean, I'm just thinking about your health; I'm old enough to say quite frankly I've outgrown pride and all those other silly provocations to marital conflict. But I do wonder sometimes, Edwina, I really do. Where do you find these guys, anyway? Do you actually go *looking* for lowlifes, or is it just that lowlifes are irresistibly attracted to you?" Sometimes Edwina made Dazzle feel extraordinarily weary and discomposed, and despondently he would root through his remembered past trying to unearth some forgotten scrap of nostalgia. He tried to formulate romantic images of himself back then, the lone roamer seeking truth in the world, learning about himself and his fellow dogs. But the romantic images rarely held together for more than a few moments at a time. When push came to shove, Dazzle had to admit it was much warmer sleeping in the trash can when Edwina was there.

EVEN THOUGH DAZZLE had tried to explain contraception to Edwina about a million times, she never once paid him a moment's notice, and in May during her second month of term Dazzle decided they should head north, into the high, unpaved country where Edwina's litter could at least expect a few simple years of the reflective life before they were meaninglessly smashed beyond recognition by some errant and uncomprehending bus. "Sometimes it's not the lived life that matters at all," Dazzle told them. They were blind and sucking and crawling all over one another, still marked by bits of unlicked blood and placenta. Edwina lay deflated and insensible in the bole of a large tree that Dazzle had padded with leaves and a few scraps of charred blanket he had discovered near an abandoned campsite. They were living in Big Sur overlooking the rough Pacific, the gnarled and wind-shaped elms and shore. "The lived life's just a con too," Dazzle told them. "Events, possessions, sights, sounds, travel, achievement–oh, and what's the famous one–oh yeah, *experience*. It's all a big cultural snow job, if you ask me. It's primitive accumulation, the myth of the entrepreneur. There aren't any entrepreneurs anymore, kids. There's just ITT, Mobil and General Dynamics—and you know what they thrive on, don't you? War, slaughtered and commodified animals like us, economic and political repression. Us unincorporated just have to do our best to carve out our own little alternative pockets of living. That's why the family's so important. I guess what I'm trying to say about all this nonsense is simply try and be happy with your life and don't worry too much about *experiencing* it. Let's all relax and enjoy ourselves. Let's find a nice long pause together, and not be in such a damn rush to get anywhere or do anything." The squirming pups just squealed and sucked. During those first few days, Dazzle felt like he was the one who had just been born.

IF THERE WAS such a thing as happiness, Dazzle thought he had found it. The role of patriarch fitted him quite snugly, and he realized that even if he could not find any sort of subjective comfort for himself he could at least meticulously envelop Edwina and her pups in comfort's illusion, that long, slow dream of culture Dazzle had always examined but never successfully comprehended before. It was Edwina's last litter, and since she didn't desire to get fucked that much anymore they were able to construct a relatively stable family environment. The pups grew with sudden and frightening alacrity, and there always seemed to be one or two of them pulling at Dazzle's tail or pawing at Dazzle's face. Dazzle hardly slept at all anymore, and generally preferred this dulled, unquenched fuzziness of brain and perception. It's best to keep the old brain a little blurred, a little battered, Dazzle decided. He had cleared out a small cave underneath an outcrop of black igneous rock on a mountainside. As the pups grew, he trained them to maintain a system of revolving security watches around their home, and drilled them in defensive techniques and maneuvers.

"A man?" he asked them.

"Hide," they said.

"Wolf?"

"Submit."

"Bear?"

"Run."

"Inexpressible sadness?"

"Run."

"Restless, unhappy dreams?"

"Dream again."

Often in the middle of Dazzle's patient drills, while the addled and hyper pups were growing distracted by buzzing flies and high birds, Edwina snuck up behind Dazzle and took a quick, nasty bite out of his ass.

"Jesus Christ!" Dazzle said.

THERE WAS A smooth diurnal rhythm to life now, Dazzle thought. You could feel the safe beat of the entire world in your blood, your heart, your dreams. Half-asleep at the mouth of their cave, he liked to listen to Edwina and the pups snoring and contemplate the stars again. Pisces, Cassiopeia, Ursa Major and of course the craters and mountains of a vast and irreproachable moon. This is where the cycle ends, he thought, if a cycle it is. It's that convergence of stars and blood, moon and heart. It's not the vain world of men. It's not the Davenports' smelly garage. It's not Dingus urinating on everything. It's not clinical depression, or obsessive, convoluted thinking. It's not even barking at the mailman.

There were still days when Dazzle would slip off to the nearest town and check out the newspapers. Islamic fundamentalism, AIDS, the international debt crisis, yuppie liberals, adamant right-wing perjurers. It's not to disavow the world that I've left it, Dazzle thought, and made his mark on the *Examiner*'s Op Ed page. It's to live in the world I've always disavowed. If he moved quickly, he could pull a nice steak from the grocery's refrigerated cabinet and sneak quietly out the back door like some innocuous delivery boy.

Periodically, though, Edwina grew ill and somewhat disaffected, lying alone for days at a time gazing insensibly at the blue sky beyond their tidy and self-sufficient cave. "Melancholy," Dazzle wondered. "Sad reflections. Lost love. Dead friends." But Edwina never told him what was on her mind; she just growled distantly. She never even bit him anymore, and eventually Dazzle realized she was suffering from physical rather than merely philosophical distress. The whites of her eyes were sallow and bloodshot. Her breath was bad, and she suffered frequent diarrhea. Small rashes formed occasionally on her back and stomach, and eventually Dazzle diagnosed a low-grade infection, perhaps septicemia, or a common form of gastroenteritis. Dazzle recalled the secret library of antibiotics he had so smugly discarded behind the water heater in the Davenport garage. You can't go back and change things, he thought. He liked that world better now, the simple one of medicine.

Early on a Monday morning Dazzle descended to town with Flaubert, the laconic and reserved pup who, like his brothers and sisters, was really a pup no longer. Flaubert was developing assurance and a quick stride. There was something wild about Flaubert that Dazzle didn't understand, something that Flaubert had either inherited from his mother or his uncivil upbringing. It wasn't just his eyes, for he carried a certain alertness in the very poise of his musculature. "The world's crisis is a crisis of representation," Dazzle explained as they descended the mountain. "We're always *representing* our lives one way or another. We're never *living* them. We never even live them *as* representations, which is an idea I've been giving a lot of thought to recently."

Alpine was a minimal town that contained a small grocery, a pharmacist's, an abandoned movie theater, a Woolworth's (which had recently been converted into a Bill's Jumbo Discount House) and approximately six hundred people. "There's a hidden continuity between signs and things, thoughts and world. Our fears of discontinuity are a fiction, actually, but one which we must be maintaining for some reason. Our anxieties about the world, things, other people, a world that doesn't conform to our dreams of it. We're letting those anxieties determine our world. Instead we should determine the world for ourselves." Coolly, Flaubert loped along like a wolf; he didn't say anything. Dazzle thought Flaubert was starting to look a little bit like Warren Oates in *The Wild Bunch*. "They're anxieties because we can't admit the validity of our dreams," Dazzle continued aimlessly. "That's what the world keeps telling us, and that's what makes us so goddamn miserable. We believe what we're told, even when we're told to believe in everything but ourselves. I'm not trying to sound like some adolescent solipsist or anything, Flaubert. I'm not saying we should deny the world. I'm just saying, let's give our dreams half a chance, too. Let's maintain some faith not only in the world but in our dreams of it."

They had come to a stop across the street from the Mercury Pharmacy, where the pharmacist, a tall man named Steve who wore a white jacket and patent leather shoes, was outside on the front curb training his guard dog, a large mean-looking Doberman whom the pharmacist referred to as Dutch, but who referred to himself in his most secret thoughts as Jasmine. The pharmacist pulled sternly at the Doberman's gleaming stainless-steel choke collar; at the same time he showed the captive dog a handful of chicken biscuits. "Sit," the pharmacist demanded, and gave the collar another sudden pull. "Sit, Dutch."

"Chicken biscuit," the Doberman said. "Chicken biscuit biscuit."

"Sit. Sit *down*, Dutch. *Sit*!" the pharmacist said.

"Maybe he doesn't want to sit," Dazzle said out loud, but nobody in the entire world was listening. "Maybe he just wants his goddamn chicken biscuit. Maybe he just wants to eat his goddamn chicken biscuit and then take a nice long nap."

When Dazzle was a puppy his favorite television program had been called *Lassie* and had starred an attractive Scottish collie who saved members of the human family she lived with each week from various life-threatening situations. Lassie dived into raging rivers and burning buildings. She stood up against wild bears and men with guns. Lassie was a brave dog, Dazzle had thought, but an exceptionally foolhardy dog as well. "Save yourself," Dazzle cried weakly, whimpering under his breath at the terrible trials and misfortunes endured by brave dogs everywhere. "Run like hell. Timmy can take care of his damn self."

"Sit," the pharmacist repeated. It was a warm day, with only a few high white clouds. "Sit *down*."

The less I understand, the simpler everything becomes, Dazzle thought, and at his signal, Flaubert took off and broke the pharmacist's grip on the Doberman's collar like a sprinter breathlessly striking the victory ribbon.

"Cats!" Flaubert cried, dashing off down the street. "We gotta catch us some cats!" The Doberman, with a brief flickering expression like the lens of a camera, poised and then, with a sudden start, took off after Flaubert. The pharmacist took off after him.

"Sit!" the pharmacist shouted, running and shaking his gleaming choke collar at the bright sky. "Heel! Stop! Sit!"

Without a moment's hesitation, Dazzle loped into the pharmacist's office, found the Prescription Out tray, and snapped up one hundred capsules of 250mg tetracycline and fifty 100mg erythromycin. Then, with a flourish, he ascended again into the high mountains.

SCOTT BRADFIELD

2 DAZZLE REDUX

DESPITE THE BURRS and bad weather, Dazzle lived a good life in the woods. He ate plenty of fresh fruit and vegetables, took one day at a time, and raised the gangly pups of his common-law wife Edwina with as much genuine affection as if they were his very own. There were times, however, when he found that being a decent father figure required more patience than he could muster. And no matter how hard he tried to restrain himself, he couldn't stop telling everybody what to do.

"No, no, *no*," Dazzle told the twins for about the zillionth time that morning. "Let's try it again, okay? *This* is a rectangle. *This* is a rhomboid. And *this* is a circle." Dazzle sketched the shapes in the powdery red dirt as he spoke them, trying to show the twins that geometry was as graspable as any bone, stick or rock. "Okay, Heckle, it's your turn. Let's pretend I've sent you on a top-secret assignment. You're supposed to go down to the Land of Men and bring me a Frisbee. Have you got that, Heckle? Do you know what a Frisbee is?"

Heckle, who had been warming his cold nose under Jeckle's gravid belly, sat up with a start. He licked his wet lips hungrily.

"Just show me the Frisbee," Heckle snapped. "I'll whip that sucker out of the sky, no problem."

"Okay, boy," Dazzle continued. "Now take a deep breath and examine the shapes I've drawn. And tell me–which one's the shape of a Frisbee? Show me the circle. The circle is the *shape* of a Frisbee. Point to the circle and you win the game."

Dazzle spoke evenly in short, compact sentences, as if he were marking a trail with bright red beads. But no matter how clearly Dazzle pointed the way, Heckle never managed to keep up.

"A circle is *like* a Frisbee?" Heckle wondered out loud, mewling and starting to twitch. "But *not* a Frisbee, really? A circle's a space on the ground when a Frisbee's not there? So what the hell do I want with a circle? Why can't I have a Frisbee instead?"

"You're thinking too hard, Heckle," Dazzle said. "Relax, take a deep breath, and point to the circle. You can do it, boy. So do it for me now."

"This is *not* the Frisbee," Heckle declared with a pounce. "Here it's *not*! This *isn't* it *here*!" Heckle was so slavery with confusion that he looked as if he had just chewed a frog. Within moments he had pawed the rhomboid completely out of existence–both metaphorically and literally.

Times like these Dazzle felt like wandering down to PCH and hurling himself in front of the first eighteen-wheeler that came along.

"Not quite, Heckle," Dazzle pronounced finally, with all the parental patience he could muster. "But at least you pointed to a geometric figure, and not a

24

dead beetle, like last time. So what say we sleep on it and take another shot in the morning. As I've said many times before–Nietzsche's *Genealogy of Morals* wasn't written in a day."

"MAYBE I'M NOT all I should be in the family skills department," Dazzle confessed that night to his erstwhile mate, Edwina. "But getting through to those kids of yours is like conversing with a block of wood, I swear. If I try to instruct them in the most basic math and science skills, they're not interested. If I try to teach them which way to look when crossing the street, they're still not interested. If I try to point out the most obvious cultural contradictions of multinational capitalism, why, forget about it. They're *really* not interested. If you can't eat it or fuck it, it's not important; that's *their* attitude. And want to know what pisses me off most? They may be *right*. Maybe fucking and eating really are the *ne plus ultra* of canine development. And in the long run of history, *I'm* the biggest fool in town."

Edwina was a pretty faithful bitch (at least since menopause), who had provided Dazzle everything he considered crucial to a long-term relationship. She never questioned (nor paid much attention to) his judgment. She rarely bit him hard enough to draw blood. And she never once kicked him out of bed for snoring. At the same time, Edwina wasn't the sort of dog who knew how to hold up her end of a conversation. In fact, whenever Dazzle started pouring out his most heartfelt anxieties, she promptly curled into a fetal ball and fell asleep.

"Growwwl," Edwina muttered, her half-lidded eyes flickering out the weird morse of dreams.

"Wolves aren't welcome 'round these parts. And neither are you mailmen."

Nevertheless, Dazzle found something comforting about a good night's sleep with Edwina. Her ambient heat soothed the knots in his shoulders, and her inattention dissolved the perplexities in his brain. As a result, Dazzle awoke every morning filled with fresh intentions and resolve.

"I'm going to be more understanding and thoughtful," Dazzle would assure himself, performing his ablutions in the piney-smelling creek. "And I won't be so quick to lose my temper." But once Dazzle had shaken himself dry with a few soul-rattling shivers and climbed back up the flinty hill, all resolutions vanished with the breeze. He saw his lazy foster-progeny licking themselves around the extinguished campfire. He smelled the unburied heaps of sour bones and dead mice. And he heard the casual yips of random lovemaking fill the rough-hewn settlement with an ambient hum. ("Roll over, sweetheart," or "You kids go chase a gopher or something. Mom and I need a little alone time—dig?") If there was one thing that really got Dazzle's dander up, it was watching his fellow dogs take the best things in life for granted, such as liberty, well-stocked provisions, and properly functioning reproductive organs.

"Come on, guys!" Dazzle barked. "Wake up and smell the coffee, will you? You can't lie around in your own filth all day. Let me show you how to rebuild that fire, or gather blueberries, or compose a sestina. I mean, what good is all this free time if you don't know how to use it? And that means *you*, Heckle, so don't go skulking into those bushes. I want you to sit down right this minute and draw me a parabola. You're gonna learn your basic geometry, pal, or my name ain't Dazzle."

OVER SUCCEEDING and weeks, Dazzle tried counting to ten, positive thinking, and just plain walking away. But no matter how much he held back, he couldn't go ten minutes without bossing his fellow dogs into a tizzy. Pretty soon the role of benevolent despot became as confining to Dazzle as any basement garage or backyard fence. And Dazzle, who couldn't bear the notion that he might be denying anybody (especially himself) true freedom, decided it was time to take another trip into the world.

"Basically," Dazzle told his assembled foster-progeny on the day he left for L.A., "I want you guys to stick together until I get back. Try not to eat so much red meat, keep an eye on your crazy mom, and don't let the pups go wild on you. Jeckle—stop hanging with coyotes. Stan—if you took a bath every few days, that rash of yours would clear up, no problem. And if for some reason I don't return from my ridiculous search or inner peace, I want you all to know that I love you, and I'm sorry I've been so temperamental these past few months. There're still a few things I need to figure out in my life, and if I don't figure them out now, I probably never will. Oh, and one last thing. I've hidden the Cheetos under a blue log by the river, so do me a favor…"

But before Dazzle could complete his final instructions, the entire clan of foster pups and grand pups took off in one shaggy, collective flash. Without even a woof good-bye, they disappeared over the first low rise and were gone.

Dazzle tried not to feel hurt or disappointed. Dogs, after all, were dogs. And by their very nature, dogs will do anything for a Cheeto.

"Try to save a few till I get back," Dazzle concluded wistfully through the swirling haze of dandruffy dog hairs. "Those name-brand snack foods don't grow on trees."

"I GUESS I'M what you'd call your basic stay-at-home individual," Dazzle's dad confessed on the morning his estranged son appeared on his doorstep. "I like to sleep every night on the same blanket, make my daily rounds pissing on the same posts, and pretty much eat out of the same garbage cans every day of my existence. And with the exception of the occasional bitch in heat that staggers my way, the high point of my life is a really good bowel movement. Rock hard, intact, clean cut at both ends. I mean, what else *is* there? Sure, I sowed my share of wild oats. But now I just want to be left alone with my memories, my naps, and my happy scrounging in alleyways and garbage cans. Which, by the way, brings me to my next point, Mr. Doozle. Or did you say your name was Dizzle?"

"Dazzle," Dazzle replied weakly, trying not to look hurt.

"Whatever. Way I look at it, maybe you could step back from my doorway just a tad. Not that I actually *doubt* your claim of kinship, mind you. But turn around slowly, that's it, keep your paws where I can see them…"

Times like this, Dazzle didn't feel embarrassed for himself. He felt embarrassed for his entire species.

"Ah, yes," Dazzle's dad said, sniffing around his

son's private parts like a pig rooting out truffles. "That's *definitely* a smell I recognize."

"Things happened at the pound, Pop. You never gave me a chanced to explain."

But of course it was already too late. Dazzle's dad emitted an abrupt snort of amazement and fell back, plop, onto his gray, flat haunches. His ice-cold nostrils flared.

"Jesus Christ, son. Somebody chopped off your balls!"

Dazzle sighed with a sad little shiver.

"Tell me about it," Dazzle said.

POP INVITED DAZZLE to spend the night in his home–the basement of a condemned Pizza Hut–and even offered to share some of his moldier blankets and food stuffs. But he refused to acknowledge any moral responsibility for Dazzle's life, or manifest the slightest degree of remorse.

"One thing I simply won't allow," Pop said, "and that's for you to make me feel bad about myself. Life's a mess, whichever way you look at it, and us dogs got to do anything we can to survive. Sometimes it means sucking up to human beings. Other times it means turning our backs on one another. In a better world, son, sure, I'd have stuck around, taught you a few things, provided for you and your sisters the best I knew how. But the world doesn't always allow us to do what we're supposed to. Sometimes we have to settle for what we *must* do instead."

"So why didn't you keep an eye on us, Pop?" Dazzle asked his father from time to time. "We were right down the street, living in that hole Mom dug behind the Lucky Market. All you had to do was walk down the street and say hello."

Dazzle's dad issued sighs like exclamations. He wasn't trying to make points, exactly. He was expressing the hard, breathy futility of saying anything at all.

"Your mom didn't want me around, sport. It would've only upset her."

"But what about after Mom went away? Why didn't you come visit then?"

"Because by that point you didn't want to see me anymore. And besides, I'd taken up with this wild bitch from Vanowen. You wouldn't have wanted me to abandon my responsibilities to her, would you?"

Sometimes, when Dazzle's inquiries grew bristly, Pop would shut off every avenue to discourse with a generic injunction. "No use rehashing the same refried beans," he might say. Or even: "Why don't we call it a day, son, and talk about it in the morning?"

DAZZLE'S DAD HAD grown so radically dissociated from his own feelings over the years that he didn't have any idea what terrible shape he was really in. He rarely bathed or picked up after himself. He ate nothing but day-old junk food foraged from back alley bins. And he never listened to a single word anybody tried to tell him, especially if it might do him any good.

Every morning Dazzle's dad woke at dawn, lapped dirty water from a blocked drain, and set off for his diurnal scrounge. Meanwhile, Dazzle trailed along dutifully like a cynical Boswell.

"Well, what have we here?" Dazzle's dad would proudly proclaim, as if he had just discovered the Northwest Passage. "Looks to me like a good-sized chunk of a double bacon cheeseburger, with a few crispy fries still attached to this melted cheese here, mmm. And if I remember correctly, son, you said we shouldn't even look in this can, right?"

Or: "Let's face it. Dogs are stupid, and humans aren't. That's why dogs live in ditches and eat garbage, and humans live in classy homes and can visit the McDonald's drive-through any damn time they please. I'm not trying to blow my own trumpet, kid, but you and I are rocket scientists compared to your normal dog. So complain all you want about my lousy child-rearing techniques. Without my brains, you'd have ridden off with the first dogcatcher that showed you a cheesy biscuit. Just like your poor stupid mom."

Or, "Let's wander past this empty lot for a moment and see... ah, there he is. Inside that sewer drain resides Mad Dingo Dog, most completely unreasonable creature I've ever known. Best if you stay out of this neighborhood altogether, son. Lesson number one of urban living is don't worry about the humans. Keep a lookout on your fellow dogs."

DEAR EDWINA,

> If you could read and I could write, I'd probably send you a letter much like the one you're holding in your paws right now.

> Visiting Dad has turned out to be a total bummer. In fact, I've never met anybody so shut down and disaffected in my life. All Dad does these days is eat chocolate doughnuts, sleep, and evade the local dogcatcher.

> I hope everybody is okay with you and the kids. Despite my frequently cranky moods, I really miss my life with you in the woods. And I

sure hope you'll all still be there when I get back.
　　Love,
　　Dazzle

DESPITE ALL HIS talk about freethinking individualism and so forth, many years of bad faith had worn Pop's identity down to the nub. If he wasn't ranting about the SPCA or the poor quality of corporate-produced fast-franchise doughnuts, he just lay motionless on the concrete floor of his hovel for hours, staring morosely at the cobwebby pointillism of dead flies on the wall.

"What's bothering you, Pop?" Dazzle would ask, testing his dad for movement the same way curious children poke dead rabbits with a stick. "What are you thinking about? Want to let me in on the big secret?"

"Nothing at all, son. Nothing I can't deal with, anyway."

"Don't you get lonely sometimes? Locked up in your own head like that?"

"Life is something you get through one day at a time, son. Stiff upper lip and all that."

"Why don't you try talking about it, Pop? When I'm feeling blue, I talk to Edwina, and it helps. Even when she doesn't understand a single word I'm trying to say."

"Talking about things doesn't make them better," Dazzle's dad replied simply, closing his eyes and scratching serenely behind one ear. "Now, if you don't mind, it's time for my afternoon nap."

Some days Dazzle felt as if he were sniffing around the perimeter of a vast, black moat filled with man-eating crocodiles. In the center of the moat stood a tall, brooding castle, elaborate with Gothic statues and hand-carved paraphernalia. Dazzle knew his dad was standing in the middle of this castle, waiting for someone to let him out. But it was impossible to let Dad *out* until someone showed Dazzle the way *in*.

Then one afternoon Dazzle went for a lonely walk through the streets of his remote, blissless puppyhood. Fences, walls, garbage bins, stray auto parts, oil-stained asphalt, bricked-over windows, and board-hammered doorways. So far as Dazzle could figure, the civilized world was filled with tacky diversions that led you into places you didn't want to go. It was like being lost in a maze where every juncture was rigged with electric wires—zap, zap. Every choice was a bad choice. And every time you made a bad choice you felt it was all your fault.

"Too much dualism," Dazzle decided, "can drive anybody nuts. Even a fairly intelligent individual like Pop."

Eventually Dazzle found himself loitering outside the ramshackle hut of Dad's weird neighbor, Mad Dingo Dog, and wondering if anybody was home. Dazzle was beginning to miss the company of other dogs, even if they weren't very bright or loquacious. At least Edwina and the kids speak the truth as clearly as their crude tongues allow, Dazzle reflected. But these shut-down alpha types like Pop, Jesus. Give me a break.

Dazzle was so mired in his reflections that he didn't notice he was no longer alone. At first he just felt the hairs bristling on his neck. Then, with an involuntary growl, he looked up.

Mad Dingo Dog had a warty, prolonged face

tufted with gray whiskers. He squinted at Dazzle for a moment, then took a perfunctory sniff at the intervening air.

"Why, I'll be a pussy's uncle," Mad Dingo Dog exclaimed. "You smell just like my long-lost nephew, Dazzle!"

THE WEIRD THING was, Dazzle didn't even know he had an uncle. And yet from the moment they met, they caught on like a house afire.

"Yeah," Mad Dingo Dog confessed, "your old man's a real piece of work. But one thing's certain—he's always been real proud of you. 'My son got himself out of this rat race,' he's always bragging. 'My son was too good for this dump, so he split. My son this and my son that.' Jeez, the old fart never stops talking about you. So what are you doing back in the Valley, for Christ's sake? I heard you had your own condo in the woods, soapy hot tub and everything. And you were running the world's first all-canine high-tech retail outlet, or something crazy like that."

Hearing all this exaggerated gossip made Dazzle feel meager by comparison. After all, Dazzle didn't want to talk about himself. Dazzle wanted to talk about *him*.

"Maybe I misunderstood what Dad was saying," Dazzle ventured after a while, "but the way he tells it, he and I are the only halfway intelligent dogs on the planet. And you're this crazy, rabid guy who howls at the moon and keeps trying to steal his best doughnuts."

Mad Dingo Dog couldn't help smiling. It resembled an allergic twitch.

"Yeah, well," Mad Dingo Dog concluded wistfully.

"That certainly sounds like your old man, doesn't it?"

BY THE TIME Dazzle returned to Dad's condemned basement, he found a dogcatcher's van parked in the alley, and a pale, overweight dogcatcher leaning into Dad's doorway with a cheesy biscuit.

"Come here, old soldier," the dogcatcher was saying, "and I'll take you to the land of milk and honey. Free chow, plenty of furry friends to keep you company, and at the end of the day, a bonus injection of this really fine medication I've put aside especially for you. No more loneliness, bud. No more wondering what it's all about. So come along, boy, that's a good dog, one more step, then another. Come get your cheesy biscuit. Then I'll drive you to the pound and teach you what real peace is all about."

In back of the idling white van a mangy assortment of alley strays were scrambling all over one another trying to get out. They yelped and howled and woofed and barked.

"Don't listen to him, guy!" an old gray bulldog cried, pawing the grated window. "It's hell in here! Whenever they're trying to kill you, they *always* offer you a cheesy biscuit!"

Dazzle contemplated this weird scenario for a moment. His dad, the dogcatcher, strays in a van, and the hot Encino sun staring implacably down. He could barely hear Dad's whisper through the distant swish of traffic on 101.

"I don't want it to hurt," Dad whispered, his nose beginning to emerge from the doorway. "I just want to go somewhere I don't have to think or feel guilty. And where nothing that happens is ever my fault."

"We'll give you oodles of peace and quiet, old

boy," the dogcatcher replied softly. He spoke with the glib confidence of a man who really liked his job. "We'll take you to a place where you don't have to think about anything anymore."

"I thought I'd leave my apartment to my son. He doesn't want me around anyway. I'm starting to get on his nerves."

For a brief moment, Dazzle thought that this was probably the sort of decision his dad should make for himself. But being a civil libertarian, he couldn't stand to see the public service sector impinging on anybody's personal freedom. So without pondering the situation further, Dazzle trotted over to the municipal-issue van, climbed into the driver's seat, and activated the emergency release with his paw. Behind him in the cabin, the hairy clamor ceased.

Then, with a faint clang, the rear doors swung miraculously open.

"I don't know about you guys," the bulldog interposed, "but I'm outta here."

Wild dogs poured from the back of the van like marbles from the mouth of a jar, ricocheting off one another in every direction. The dogcatcher was so startled that he dropped his cheesy biscuit.

"Wait! Stop! Bad dog! Bad dog!" He was issuing shotgun proclamations and running down the alley. Eventually he turned the far corner and disappeared.

"Bad dogs to *you*, maybe," Dazzle said. "But to my way of thinking, they're just doing what dogs gotta do."

THAT NIGHT, AFTER a lackluster celebratory bash of chocolate doughnuts and Diet Tab, Dazzle finally told his dissociative old dad the news.

"I'm sorry, Pop," he said, "but I can't stand to see you do this to yourself anymore. I had these illusions, right, that maybe we'd reach some sort of reconciliation, and maybe you'd even come home with me to the woods and help raise your grandchildren. But now I realize you're so tied up in your endless routines and bad faith that you'll never let go. So what I'll do, see, is tell the grandkids you died. I'll tell them you sent your love, but that you rolled over and died shortly after I found you. You got hit by a car, or developed lung cancer from this ridiculous smog, or got shot in the butt by some soiled kid with a BB gun. I'll use you as an example, Pop, of what urban America can do to a dog, and if we're lucky, maybe none of our semi-progeny will ever stumble into this hellhole you can't seem to leave. I won't kiss you good-bye or anything, but just say thanks for your hospitality and get my poor frazzled butt out of here. If I start now, I can maybe hit Ventura by morning."

Dazzle finished having his say with an expiring sigh. Ahh, Dazzle thought, I wasn't even angry or anything. I just needed to tell him good-bye.

"So what is it, Pop?" Dazzle asked from the verge of the weedy doorway. Dazzle was wearing a painstakingly adjusted backpack slung over one shoulder; it contained a cheese sandwich, a stale jelly doughnut, and a half-liter bottle of Evian. "Am I taking off and you've got nothing left to say? Don't lose the moment, Pop. I've lost a few moments in my life and I can promise you one thing: you don't get them back."

Dazzle's dad regarded his son with a slightly cocked expression, as if he heard distant birds singing.

Then, for the first time in his life, he finally told Dazzle what was really on his mind.

"Grandkids?" Dazzle's dad said. "You never told me about grandkids."

SO DAZZLE TOOK his dad home to the high mountains, where they never exchanged any true, heartfelt words ever again. After all, there's plenty of sunshine and fresh air to keep you occupied in the mountains. And sometimes talk just gets in the way of living.

"I guess I'll never be a perfect father," Dazzle confided to Edwina one night, gazing out at the star-littered sky. "Or even a perfect son, for that matter. And when I die, there may not be another dog in the entire world who knows how to light the evening fire, or record the day's events for posterity. But history belongs to each generation to figure out for itself, so there's no point in me getting all worked up about things I can't change. Sometimes, old girl, a dog needs to stop wrestling with the world long enough to get on with the simple fact of living in it. Like you and me, Edwina. Living together–nose to haunch and haunch to nose."

It was a miraculous summer that Dazzle would remember fondly all his life. The pups grew progressively leaner, brighter, and more independent. Brisk sea winds kept the white sun cool. And wild wolves occasionally drifted into the orbit of their encampment, lured by aromas of toasted marshmallows and bitches in heat. It was a summer of perfect somnolence and irreflection. Except, of course, when it came to Dazzle's immutable dad.

"For crying out loud!" Dazzle's dad was often

heard exclaiming through the warm, fir-scented air. "It's a *rhomboid*, for Christ's sake! Don't you idiots know what a *rhomboid* is?"

But it was one of the miracles of that particular summer that nobody ever figured out what a rhomboid was. Nobody even cared.

3 DAZZLE'S INFERNO

ON A BLEAK November afternoon, while searching Highway 1 for an errant grandpup, Dazzle was snapped up by the SPCA and transported to the Animal Preservation Facility in Ventura, where he was printed, tagged and impounded. "Preservation, *hah*, that's a laugh," Dazzle thought out loud as he was corralled into a mesh-wire compound. "Elimination of unreliable elements—*that's* more like it." By the time the shock wore off, Dazzle found himself immured by hypersanitary living conditions, cold-eyed animal welfare agents, and just about the sorriest collection of fellow mutts he had ever encountered.

"So I don't get it," Dazzle opined to anybody who would listen. "They deworm and delouse us, shoot us full of antibiotics, and when they think we're healthy enough, they throw us into this steel trap where we're expected to piss through the floors and drink out of rusty bowls. I mean, just look at this bedding, for Christ's sake. Is that a vinyl bean-bag chair or what? It's not comfort they're aiming for. It's something you can hose down, turn over, and reuse."

41

But rather than acknowledge his admittedly wrong-footed efforts at communication, Dazzle's fellow inmates either growled him away from their Nibbles or tried to mount him from behind and fuck him in the bottom.

Hey!" Dazzle yelped, shaking free from the latest serial perv with a hippy little snap. "You're barking up the wrong sycamore, bud. Nothing personal, either. It's just the way I happen to roll."

EVERYWHERE DAZZLE TURNED, his cellmates were engaged in closet-busting activities, as if the very meaning of privacy had been turned inside out. They freely licked themselves and one another in every conceivable orifice, poohed in the water bowl and dry-humped the bedding. And at the drop of a hat, they fought fiercely over nothing, gouging and clawing and gnashing and shredding.

"If I told you once I told you a thousand times—stay away from my Nibbles!"

"Don't look at me that way or even think what you're thinking!"

"What's oozing from that pustule? Do you mind? Mmm, thanks. I needed that."

"Hate me hate me hate me hate."

There were times when Dazzle felt like a bit of meat hurled into the gasketed vortices of some mighty machine—a process for producing pies, say, or a sharply pronged chicken defeatherer. Everything that was most mindless about dogs had been amplified out of all proportion until all you could hear was the raucous metal whine of denaturized stuff: bile, testosterone, greed, fear, denial and rage.

"You guys are the end of language," Dazzle told

them, curled up with disbelief in a corner. "You guys are the end of rational thought. At this point we should be banding together, singing songs to bolster our spirits, and raging against the darkness. It's supposed to be us against them; but with you guys, it's everybody against each other, raw in tooth and claw. Believe me, you guys gotta think straight for a minute and make a choice. Either work to a common purpose or die alone. It's up to you."

"WHERE ARE THE puppies, Daddy?"

"They're in another pen, sweetheart. These are the grown-up doggies. The ones that got lost from their masters and nobody wants."

"Can we see the puppies now?"

"It never hurts to look, sweetheart. Like this doggy here? He looks nice, doesn't he?"

Of all the indignities Dazzle had suffered, visiting hours took the biscuit. Every weekend afternoon, human beings in search of pliable pets were hustled past on their way to the nursery, but they never stayed long. After all, Dazzle reflected, nobody wants a self-formed dog with his own thoughts and opinions. They only want malleable, just-weaned babies they can mold into treat-mongers and guard-dogs. Dogs who take what you give them and never complain.

"I don't know, Daddy," the little girl said. "Why's he looking at me so funny?"

"What do you mean, sweetheart? He's a pretty dog and well mannered. He's just looking at you that way because—oh, I see. That is a funny expression. It's almost as if, as if…"

"It's like he doesn't like me, Daddy. But I'm not important enough to make him mad."

Bingo, Dazzle thought, gazing into the moppet's muddy brown eyes. Dazzle had never been terribly fond of human beings, but at least adults remembered to feed, water, and run you on occasion. Moppets, however, were always dressing you in doll clothes and tempting you with fast-food sandwiches and candy bars, as if you were too stupid to know twenty-four-carat crap when you saw it.

"Yes, darling, well, at least we gave the older doggies a sporting chance. Now, let me at those puppies! I think we should get a cute one and teach it all sorts of neat tricks."

"And it'll love me, won't it, Daddy? It'll love me more than anything. Even more than its own mommy!"

As the human visitors were ushered happily toward the nursery, where the pulse-pleasing cacophony of puppies filled the air like Muzak, Dazzle sighed with relief.

"My mommy was a neurotic bitch who lived behind a Dumpster," Dazzle thought after them, with that sense of quiet grandeur that only comes to those without hope. "And for the record, Chickie—you'll never take the place of *my* mommy."

THEY WERE ALL riding the same short conveyor belt to nowhere.

"You're tagged with this number, right? Around your neck. There, right *there*," Dazzle explained to the only dog who paid attention, a mixed wire-hair spaniel named Grunt with weird rubbery growths on his face. "And this number corresponds to the date you were processed, see? And when your thirty days are up, so are you. Poof. In South America, you've entered the ranks of los *desaparecidos*. And once that happens, it's like you've never been born."

Grunt was an unusually curious dog, part border collie on his father's side, who could sit for hours watching words issue from Dazzle's lips like glistening soap bubbles.

"You talk and I'll listen," Grunt steadfastly assured Dazzle. "It's like I got this reverse attention-deficit thing going, *comprende*? I gotta keep staring at somebody or I go totally nuts."

In many ways, Grunt was the perfect friend for a dog like Dazzle, who liked to talk but wasn't so wild about listening.

"Human civilization is like this big machine, right?" Dazzle continued, inspired by Grunt's unwavering attention. "Turning everything we are into everything we're not. Surplus value, commodities, spin, psychobabble, culture, landfill, graphs. To creatures like that, we aren't dogs. We're just a record of human efficiency, a pie chart to be displayed at the next managerial review. How quickly we were eliminated–that'll matter. How cost-efficiently we were incinerated–that'll matter too. But the moral and philosophical reasoning behind why we were destroyed in the first place, well, nobody will waste too much time on *that*. Those aren't the sort of questions that can be submitted with your next budget proposal. If you want to build yourself a nice golden parachute, you'd better leave those questions alone."

"Absitively!" Grunt yipped. "Posolutely!" Grunt was so deeply affirmative that he glowed. "Tell it like it is, Dazzle! I could listen to you all night!"

Sometimes Grunt was so exhaustively attentive

that Dazzle actually ran out of things to say. He looked at Grunt looking at him and eventually lay down on the cold mesh floor, closed his eyes, and felt Grunt's intensity drilling through the back of his neck.

"Are you going to sleep?" Grunt asked wonderingly. "Well, okay, you know where to find me. Sometimes I take these little naps with my eyes open, I don't even know it's happening. So don't be startled, Dazzle, if you wake up to find me already here."

ON THE SAME rainy afternoon that the ward's biggest bullies, Spike and Fatso, were led to the dispensary yipping "Snacks! Bitches! Sunlight! Snacks!" an especially bland, perspicacious visitor arrived at the Adult Male Holding Facility. Her name was Dr. Harriet Harmony, and she wielded a clipboard, a severely-bitten plastic ball-point pen, and a wallet-sized electronic calculator.

"Uh oh," Dazzle told Grunt, who was chewing his toes in a way that Dazzle found particularly revolting. "I don't like the look of this babe what so ever."

Dr. Harriet Harmony had received her B.A. in animal husbandry from Princeton, and her doctorate from Iowa State. She wore sensible shoes, wire-rim bifocals and a crude, hasty bob that might have been self-administered with a prison shaving mirror and a cereal bowl.

"Vivisection," Grunt growled darkly and crawled under Dazzle's tail to hide. It was the longest word Dazzle had ever heard spoken by a dog to whom he wasn't intimately related.

"Which of you big boys would like to go with Dr.

Harmony?" asked Maggie, the floor supervisor. To get their attention, she brushed her hand across the mesh with a metallic thip-thip-thip sound, as if she were petting a huge, scaly reptile. "Guess what Dr. Harmony has waiting for you at her housy-wousy? A big bowl of meaty Alpo."

The very word struck a chill into Dazzle's heart. Whenever human beings were about to do something truly unconscionable to a dog, they always promised him Alpo.

Flipping through the forms on her clipboard, Dr. Harmony confirmed the identity of one random mutt after another with a brisk switch of her pen. Check. Check.

"Too big," she noted out loud. "Too furry. Too pure-bred. Too mean."

It's times like this you believe in precognition, Dazzle thought. From the moment Dr. Harmony appeared, he knew they were meant for each other.

"What about this one?" Dr. Harmony asked.

She wasn't looking at Dazzle. She was looking at Adult Male No. 4243.

"Oh, isn't he a *cutey*," Maggie enthused. She already had Dazzle's attention, but she wanted much more. "Would you like to take a little walk with Dr. Harmony, you big cutey-wooty? You big hairy cutey you!"

DAZZLE WAS ALLOWED no time at all to console poor Grunt, who leaped and spun fiercely as if he were being teased by a bone on a bungee cord.

"Don't worry, Grunt!" Dazzle shouted as he was pulled away down the corridor by Maggie's leather leash. "If they torture me to death for the sake of improving human deodorants, at least I'll glimpse the blue sky again on my way out! And come to think of it, who wouldn't like to see some improvement in human deodorants? I'm all for it. How about you?"

For once, Dazzle's words had a resounding effect on his fellow dogs.

"Human smells!" they barked. "How we hate those awful human smells!"

"Whatever you do, don't let them hook anything to your testicles!" Grunt shouted in dim, diminishing yips.

And Dazzle smiled over his shoulder, flattered by Grunt's concern.

"If they want to hook anything to my testicles, they'll have to call my old vet in Reseda and ask where he buried 'em. Take care of yourself, pal. And keep a tight asshole—dig?"

IT HAPPENED SO fast that Dazzle never knew what hit him. He was retagged and reregistered, driven to West Los Angeles in a minivan, and reconfined in a smaller, tidier private accommodation in the recently endowed, Egyptian-style monolith of the Center for Applied Sciences at UCLA.

"Welcome to your new home," Dr. Harmony told him and curtly disappeared with her clipboard.

The accommodation was equipped with a water dispenser, a yelp-activated shower, and, lo and behold, a fresh bowl of Alpo.

"You're not fooling me with that old trick," Dazzle grumbled, and curled up disdainfully on the floor beside the clean fragrant cotton futon, adorned with bright, squeaky rubber toys like a canine odalisque. "You guys tell me what you want, and I'll decide if I'm giving it to you."

Within the hour, Dr. Harmony returned with her senior research supervisor and a pretty young court stenographer named Carol.

"Welcome to UCLA," Dr. Marvin said slowly, as if he were addressing a roomful of multinational students in a TEFL course.

The stenographer, cued by Dr. Marvin's nonaggressive smile, began to type.

Tappety-tappety-tappety-tappety.

"We hope you are finding everything satisfactory."

Tip-tappety-tappety-tap-tappety-tap.

"And that you will graciously accept this opportunity to meet with the recently endowed Department of Animal Linguistics on an equal footing."

Tappety-tappety-tappety-tappety-tip.

"Let's put the ugly days of blood-hurling demonstrators and bad publicity behind us. With the kind and generous support of Animals Alive!, the officially registered charity of sport-shoe entrepreneur and animal-lover, R. Wallace MacShane, we are about to forge a new era in human-animal relations."

Tappety-tip-tappety-tap-tap-tap-tap. Tap.

The moment Carol stopped typing, Dr. Marvin and Dr. Harmony exchanged curt, professional smiles. Then, in one smoothly synchronized motion, they entered Dazzle's cell, crouched, and offered their hands in a gesture of olfactory openness.

Dazzle couldn't work up enough enmity to growl. Had he his druthers, he would have liked to forge a new era of human-animal relations in Dr. Harmony's fat butt.

At which point Dr. Harmony slipped one hand

into the vest pocket of her white lab coat, grabbed Dazzle by the haunch, and injected him with the largest, nastiest hypodermic he had ever seen.

"Yowzah!" Dazzle expostulated, starting to his feet as the numbness spread to his haunches, his ribs, his face, his tongue.

"You goddamn, goddamn…" Dazzle said.

And collapsed unconscious to the floor.

AS DAZZLE EVENTUALLY learned, Dr. Harmony was inspired as a young girl by the best-selling fictional reflections of a sage, beneficent ape who had many wise things to say about the meaning of life and the harmonic convergences of nature. This ape bore no grudge against the Homo saps who had enslaved him in a zoo, since he pitied their collective inability to love, or be loved, with total sincerity.

"I guess that sensitive, beautiful creature taught me everything I know about Nature," Dr. Harmony confessed, drifting beside Dazzle in the dreamily burbling laboratory. "And as a result of his patient instruction, I learned to look beyond my petty, callous concerns, and explore the spiritual oneness of Nature. I learned that this oneness invests every living creature on our planet, no matter how small, grubby or ignoble. It invests doggies, and kitties, and monkeys, and me. I want you to know that I consider you a lot more important than some silly, tenure-achieving article in *Nature* or *Biology Today*, and can only hope we won't remain divided from one another by the false dichotomy of humans-slash-animals. I'm hoping we'll learn to respect one another as *friends*."

Dazzle was not sure how long he had been drifting in the closed current of Dr. Harmony's voice. He only knew that she was with him, then she wasn't, then she was with him again.

"I guess what I'm trying to say is that we make

sacrifices every day for Mother Nature. Mainly because in difficult, war-torn times like these, Mother Nature can use all the help she can get."

WHEN DAZZLE AWOKE he found himself drifting in a huge, gelatin-filled tank in a wide, omniscient laboratory buzzing with video cameras and metabolic gauges. His eyes were sewn open; his paws were bound by see-through plastic tape. And an array of multicolored, follicular implants sprouted from his forehead like a cybernetic toupee.

"We call it a syntactical eductor," Dr. Marvin explained, standing before Dazzle's immersion tank with the rapt, wide-open stare of a child observing his first jellyfish in an aquarium. "For as you may soon understand, it's not words that generate meaning, but how those words are arranged and presented. Subject and noun, subjunctive and possessive, predicate and noun. The invisible logic that our brains weave of things, thoughts, and sensations. Deprived of semantics, we drift through a universe of disparity and contradiction. We don't know which way is up, or how far, or how to get there from here. We can't distinguish us from them, or him from her, or being from what used to be. No wonder you poor animals have such a hard time, herded mindlessly from one form of oppression to another, trapped by your limited comprehension, which can only process one thought at a time, such as Sit, Shake, Dinnertime, and Kiss-kiss. But today, Mr. Adult Male No. 4243, is the first day of the rest of your life. In receiving the Promethean gift of syntax, you will engage everything that comes with it. Such as synchronicity, intention, history, and causation."

At this point, Dr. Harmony stepped forward, holding a compact digital microphone, as if she were about to perform a high-tech karaoke.

"**Me like doggy**," Dr. Harmony enunciated, placing her flat, bitten fingernails against the glass of Dazzle's container. "**Me protect doggy. Doggy help me. Me help doggy.**"

There was something so horrific about the concentrated sincerity of Dr. Harmony's face that Dazzle couldn't bear to watch. Meanwhile, the electronically translated words clanked hollowly through his wired synapses, like chords plunked out on a child's xylophone.

His brain literally rattled with words.

"**Me talk nice to doggy**," Dr. Harmony continued, miming the removal of fragrant words from her mouth, and presenting them to Dazzle like red rubber chew toys. "**Doggy speak nice to *me*? What do you say, doggy? Me want to hear your words *very much*.**"

The inflections pinged in Dazzle's brain like the chimes of a cash register. And for the first time that Dazzle could remember, a human question mark developed into an invitation to speak.

Dazzle wished he were the sort of dog who could resist such an invitation. But, of course, he wasn't.

"Spuh," Dazzle said. His metal voice rasped on the overhead speakers like a dog chain sliding across a stainless steel bowl. "Spuh, *spuh*."

Until a miraculous, deep-timbered voice emerged into the wide laboratory like James Earl Jones announcing the divine presence of CNN:

"Spuh-spuh-spare me the condescending horse-shit, sister," Dazzle said. "And you got a lot of nerve, by the way–talking to me like *I'm* stupid."

FOR SEVEN DAYS and seven nights, Dazzle raged at the blunt world, hitting it with all the stuff he had in him: iron negativity and rage. It was a bizarrely liberating experience.

He raged at their illusions about democracy: "Okay, so every country's divided up into these two cosmetically antithetical political parties, both of which represent people with money. Isn't that what's called a tautology? Two absurdly redundant propositions. That's what your political process looks like to me, honey. A human fucking tautology."

He raged at their illusions about dogs: "Of *course* we roll over and wag our stupid tails and follow you around the house, mewling and twitching at every scrap of affection. We're *prisoners*, for Christ's sake. If we live in the basement, who will feed us? Certainly not that idiotic mailman, who shoves rolled-up newspapers through the grate. And what do rolled-up newspapers represent? Mind control, torture, irrational submission to authority. If you ask me (and I hate to remind you, but you *did* ask me, and now I'm *telling* you) that mailman deserves all the grief he can get."

And without mercy or remorse, he raged at their illusions about Nature. "So what do you tell yourself about this grand project, Dr. Harmony, alone in your bed at night? Personally, I've got you pegged as a *Dances with Wolves* girl–wow, you should have seen yourself flinch. You've probably got the Director's Cut on DVD, right? And you light all your scented candles after a hot bath in some slinky robe, and stretch out on that crummy student couch you still

53

can't afford to replace, and you *are* native woman, aren't you, Dr. Harmony? And you will purify your Kevin baby with that adorable mustache of his and that oh-so-striking uniform, waiting for him to carry you into your tepee where you will teach him the magic ways of–cool it, Dr. Harmony, okay. I'll stop. But before I do, let me tell you something about Mother Nature. She's got crabs, and lice, and about eight billion venereal infections, and every ingrown hair and toenail usually develops into this oozing, life-threatening abscess. I *am* Nature, and do I sound wise and benevolent to you? You don't have to answer that, Dr. Harmony. What you think about me is written all over your face."

And ultimately, Dazzle raged at himself: "So I developed this extended family in the woods, right, with about a thousand step-pups and step-grandpups running around, bickering and fighting all the time and copulating with anything that moves, and it feels, it feels *all right*. It feels like what you guys call really 'grown up'. And I drift off, Dr. Harmony, into my sentimental dreams of wholeness and true being, tinged with irony and all that, but isn't everything tinged with irony, whether we like it or not? I mean, there I am, trying to teach the pups about being true to themselves, and doing the best they can and so forth, and meanwhile, what's happening to the world? Are dogs receiving progressively better treatment at the hands of you and your fellow saps? Are social institutions growing more progressive and humane? Is even the notion of equality between species being knocked around by college eggheads like yourself, not because dogs and cats are that smart or anything, but we're sure not any *stupider* than you guys. And when I get my bottom tossed into that dandy little concentration camp called Animal Preservation, well, I can't help thinking I brought it on myself, and watching my fellow dogs brutalize one another in every conceivable fashion, it starts to feel like dying, Dr. Harmony. I don't know how else to explain it. Like I'm saying good-bye to every illusion I ever had about myself and my fellow dogs. I never wanted to die, Dr. Harmony, but something happened to me in the past few weeks, and these days I guess I don't much want to live, either. So now that I can say what's on my mind, it's like all I've got to say is, well, nothing. Nowhere. Nohow. I'm left to wonder what you think about all this. Me, this chattering dog in this huge fishbowl, talking your head off for seven days and seven nights. What do you think about what I'm saying, Dr. Harmony? Answer that question, and it'd be like discourse. The first step toward something bigger than us both. What do *you* think about *me*?"

No so surprisingly, Dr. Harmony missed her cue. Flanked by Dr. Marvin (who was writing a grant proposal) and the court stenographer (who was tappily transcribing the ineluctable data that was Dazzle) Dr. Harmony gazed into the translucent goo as if trying to remember where she left her car keys.

"What I think," Dr. Harmony said emptily. The pistons missed a beat, then another. "What I think. You want to know what *I* think."

Even Dr. Marvin put down his Bic. And the court stenographer, sensing a rare opportunity, reached for her warm can of diet soda to take a long, habit-quenching swallow.

"What I think is, well, I guess it's this. I think it's time for you to shut the fuck up, you stupid annoying mutt."

THEY DEACTIVATED THE recording machines, the lights, and the overhead fans, and everybody (with the obvious exception of Dazzle) went home for a well-deserved rest. It was the first time in weeks that Dazzle had an opportunity to hear himself think. "You can either talk or think," Dazzle often told his foster-pups and grandpups. "But you can't do both at the same time. It just doesn't work that way."

When Dazzle was a teething pup, he knew the meaning of words before he knew the words themselves. "Yip," he might tell Mom, shaking his nose at the blue sky. Yip: clouds. Yip: cars. Yip yip: last night I saw a blazing meteor. Yip yip *yip* yip: I love catching buzzy flies in my mouth. In many ways, the words themselves hadn't mattered; for whatever Dazzle said, Mom smiled and licked his face in reply.

I was speaking my *me*, Dazzle thought. And that's all that mattered to Mom. The language we inhabited when we lay together.

Yip, Dazzle thought now, drifting in the slow tremble of gelatin like a chunk of pineapple in a blancmange. Yip.

Flickery, unbidden images appeared on the screen of his imagination: a ball, a stick, a bowl of Nibbles. Yip. A cardboard box. Yip. A meaty bone. We speak our minds and other creatures never quite understand, Dazzle thought. Which is, I'm afraid, what language is all about.

THE FOLLOWING MORNING, Dazzle made his demands known to the first employee to reactivate the overhead lighting.

"Basically, tell Dr. Harmony I'll be issuing a list of demands at oh-nine-hundred hours, so I'd like our stenographer present. And Dr. Marvin, of course, is more than welcome to attend–though what constitutes his actual purpose around here, other than signing his name to the articles his grad students write, presently eludes me. Also, it might be time to fly R. Wallace MacShane down from Marin. He and I need to share some major face time. Oh, and one more thing. I'd like you guys to stop calling me Adult Male No. 4243. My name, if you haven't noticed, is Dazzle."

ROBERT WALLACE MACSHANE was an all-right kind of guy. He flew an energy-efficient private jet. He wore non-blend earth tone slacks, shirts, and shoes. He provided his nonunion domestic employees with a near-union-scale wage, pension scheme, and medical plan. And he always referred to his underpaid nondomestic employees as brave pioneers of the burgeoning Third World super-state.

"So here we are," Robbie said, clapping his warm, well-manicured hands together. Robbie liked to begin every *tête-à-tête* as if he were getting down to a happy weekend of dad-and-son touch football. "Dr. Marvin. Dr. Harmony. Me and, well... *you.*"

A blink was the closest Robbie ever came to a shrug.

"Our, uh, esteemed canine colleague who, through the aid of modern technology, has crossed the great cultural divide to speak to us from the hallowed, er–"

Dazzle didn't have time for this.

"Yadda-da-yadda-da," Dazzle said, eliciting a confused squeal of feedback from the overhead speakers. "Are the tapes running? They are? Then, Carol, will you begin transcribing? We should begin."

As a pup, Dazzle had spent many lazy afternoons in front of the television watching black-and-white reruns of *Thin Man* movies on *Dialing for Dollars*. In these highly unrealistic, Depression-era mysteries, William Powell and Myrna Loy wandered from one dinner party to another, uncovering corpses, making friends with heartsick young people, and getting completely tanked along the way. Then, during the closing minutes, they solved the accumulated crimes at a recitation attended by any and all surviving suspects, along with the local police chief, who couldn't catch a cold without their help. Meanwhile, their useless pooch, Asta, chewed the carpets and performed backflips like a trained bear at the circus.

This one's for you, Asta, Dazzle thought.

"So at first I figure it's just typical self-congratulation," Dazzle told them. "The victor's history lesson and all that. Big-time academics reaching down to shake the paw of lowly canines, airplay on all the networks, drive-time talk and late-night panel. Hey, before you know it, you've got your well-verbalized pooch appearing regularly on *Stupid Human Tricks*, or maybe he's one of the more lovable castaways on the next all-species edition of *Survivor*. They keep spelling your names right, and the name of this fine institution. This attracts more grants, and more notoriety, and pretty soon I'm like that sheep they cloned, that Daisy Whatever. It's not progress that matters—just the same public relations machine grinding out copy. At least dogs piss where they think it might do some good, but *you* guys. You just love the smell of yourselves, don't you? You just love to spread it around."

Robert Wallace MacShane firmly stood his ground and smiled the smile he was known for. It was the sort of smile he smiled very well indeed.

"I'm listening," he said. And for the first time that morning he took a chair beside Dr. Harmony, who was slurping Red Zinger from a hefty-sized Dr. Dolittle II promotional mug. "My conference call isn't till ten-thirty."

If Dazzle could have smiled, he would have given R. Wallace MacShane a run for his money. Instead, Dazzle leaned back in his roomy mind and produced the only emphasis at his disposal.

He *modulated*.

"Ahh," Dazzle's smoother, warmer voice said out loud.

At which point Dazzle let them have it.

"But one way or another, things don't look good for yours truly. I'm not exactly lovable or charming or telegenic. I don't do tricks on demand. And you've clearly dumped a good chunk of your endowment wiring me up to these doohickeys, with what to show for it? An irascible, anti-social canine who won't exactly be barking your praises to Rosie. Which leaves you two choices. You can perform an expensive surgical reversal, unhook and delinguify me, then suture up all these exposed nerves and whatnot. *Or* you can cut all the cables and toss me in the Dumpster. What are the odds, guys? You want to make me famous or make me dead?"

Dr. Marvin made a point of not looking at Dr. Harmony.

Dr. Harmony made a point of looking directly at Dr. Marvin.

Ha, Dazzle thought. I think we call that gin.

"Which leaves me swimming in this soup," Dazzle resumed smartly. "Wondering what I can offer you guys in exchange for my sorry bones back. And that's when I think the magic word."

Dazzle paused for effect.

"Nibbles," he said finally.

R. MacShane's smile suffered a noticeable glitch, as if his software had gone slightly ditzy.

"Nibbles," Dazzle continued. "They're the one common denominator, right? Nibbles at the Animal Preservation Center. Nibbles being pulverized by that whirring processor and pumped into my veins through these tubes. Nibbles, Inc., which is a minor subsidiary of Worldco Foods, which is itself co-proprietor of Kidco Shoes, which is controlled by a panel of stockholders appointed by the very same CEO who appoints them, and who just happens to be sitting in this room. Robbie, our golden boy. Robert Wallace MacShane."

Robbie performed a curt little bow.

"It's like some basic elemental matter, the building blocks of our universe. Not atoms or energy or karma, but Nibbles, and it comes in a variety of flavors. Barbecued Ribs. Chicken Korma. Tuna Surprise. And for those diabetic dogs, there's sugar-free Veggie-Burger Plus, with all the flavor and protein of raw meat. To hear you guys talking about Nibbles it's like you discovered the Holy Grail or something, or the latest wonder dish whipped up by Wolfgang Puck. But the fact of the matter, as any dog can tell you, is that Nibbles tastes like shit. Imagine dirt clods sprinkled with pesticides and chemicals, and you're in the same ballpark. You could soak this stuff in water for a thousand years and it would still taste like dirt clods. But what does it say on every Nibbles container ever produced in the history of this planet? It says: 'Dogs *love* 'em!' Now doesn't that make you wonder, Robbie? How you guys can produce Nibbles by the boatload and tell everybody dogs love 'em when nobody knows what dogs really love. Or, for that matter, even cares."

R. Wallace MacShane was getting his smile back, drumming his neatly manicured fingers against his knee.

"My dog loves Nibbles," Robbie insisted smugly. "You should see Rex gobble them down."

It would make me sad, Dazzle thought, if it didn't make me so angry.

"What choice do you give Rex?" Dazzle asked. "I mean, does Rex *love* Nibbles more than, say, chicken-fried steak? Try putting a bowl of salsa-flavored Nibbles next to a hunk of chicken-fried steak, Robbie, and then tell me which one Rex *really* loves best."

It all makes sense, Dazzle thought, watching the various faces watch him. Dr. Marvin: thinking about the grant appropriations committee that afternoon. Dr. Harmony: thinking about how much she loathed Dr. Marvin. And Carol, the stenographer, looking at her can of Diet Tab with a new, half-formed expression. Could she be thinking about the possible connections between Nibbles and Diet Tab?

You could never be sure who would be the first person in a room to figure out what was really going on.

Robbie's drumming fingers stilled. Like any good negotiator, he knew this was the part where the guy holding all the cards offered you the only deal in town.

"Bring me the *Yellow Pages*," Dazzle told them. "Turn them to Entertainment Lawyers and hook me to a phone line. Meanwhile, Dr. Harmony should get her skates on and hustle over to Animal Preservation, where my pal Grunt will be staring into the eye of a pretty nasty hypodermic right about now. Then, and only then, we'll talk contract."

AFTER A FEW weeks of physio, Dazzle regained most of his old poise and swagger; and once the sutures healed, he booked himself and Grunt into the Ventura Doggy Motel, where they treated themselves to a hot flea shampoo, chicken-fried steaks, and a few sharp, well-received tonguefuls of strawberry schnapps. But even after Dazzle's hair had grown back over the scar tissue, his expression retained a weird, jigsawish incongruity, as if he were looking in two directions at once.

"Every so often, life takes us apart," Dazzle told Grunt on the day they were released back into the wide world. "And if we're lucky, we live long enough to put ourselves back together again. But along the way, we lose these little pieces of ourselves, and enduring these little losses is what life is all about. Not paving ourselves over with cosmetic surgery, or spackle, or bad faith. But wearing our brokenness openly in our hearts and on our faces."

As per Dazzle's instructions, the Oldsmobile Town Car dropped them off at the intersection of PCH and Spring Valley Road. Unsurprisingly (at least to Dazzle), this intersection was marked by a self-illuminated Nibbles billboard, as big as a barn.

"Maybe I sold out, Grunt. I don't know. I've

always believed in speaking the truth as well as my crude tongue allows, but sometimes you just want your life back. You just want to save your selfish sack of bones and go home."

Dazzle and Grunt were standing on the freeway's soft shoulder, gazing up at the rumpus-room-sized bowl of multicolored Nibbles.

The billboard's caption read:

LATEST SCIENTIFIC ADVANCES CONFIRM DOGS LOOOOOOOVE NEW, IMPROVED BOLOGNESE-FLAVORED NIBBLES *MORE* THAN FRESH MEAT!

Dazzle could abide the caption. What he couldn't abide was the tiny, asterisked confirmation that ran along the baseboard like the health warning on a cigarette pack:

*THESE STATEMENTS INDEPENDENTLY CONFIRMED BY EXPERIMENTS CONDUCTED AT UCLA ANIMAL RESEARCH LABORATORIES DOCUMENTATION AVAILABLE ON REQUEST

Staring up at that monumental load of drivel, Dazzle couldn't help sighing at the enormity of language. It's we who should be speaking words, he thought. But more often than not, it's words that speak *us*.

Despite his brave face, Dazzle did not feel victorious, smug, or even clever. In fact, he didn't feel much of anything—only weakness in his heart, and the deep impress of too many years. Standing at the junction of four roads, he couldn't even decide which way to turn, or why one road might be better than any other road.

They might have sat there all day had it not been for the surprising impatience of Grunt.

"Sometimes he have to fight like hell just to keep hold of what little we've already got," Grunt said. "Wind, trees, rocks, sunlight, clouds, you name it. Not just our selfish skin, as you put it, but our genuinely selfless pleasure in everything that isn't us. The best we have to offer the world is who we really are, Dazzle. And to my mind, that's justification enough to carry on."

It was the sort of wisdom Dazzle had always aspired to, perhaps when he was older and less prone to querying. Simple, regular, heartfelt, and as true as you could make it. And here it was, just when he least expected it, coming at him through the unremarkable voice of a fellow dog.

Who would've figured?

"Someday, Dazzle, you'll stop talking long enough to listen," Grunt said gently. "Hell, who knows? You might even learn a thing or two."

At which point, Grunt showed Dazzle the quickest route out of town.

4. DAZZLE GETS POLITICAL

IT WAS A flat, wide-avenued and treeless valley town just off the main freeway, featuring a hardware store, an all-night burger joint and a bank. No more and no less than a good place to start for a dog on a mission.

"Justice?" shouted the angry, bearded man who drove up every morning in his '67 Chevy flatbed. "Well don't you wait around for justice in *this* life, little doggy! You think our government officials care about the health and well-being of a scrawny, homeless mutt like yourself? When they clearly don't care about the health and well-being of us natural-right-bipeds who elected them in the first place? All government cares about is taking away what little we working men still got. Such as our natural supremacy over women, and our constitutional right to bear fire-arms. So don't lecture *me* about justice, little doggy. 'Cause if it don't exist for human beings, it sure as hell don't exist for dogs."

Dazzle was sitting patiently on his customary street-corner with an EZ-Race Message Board propped up beside him. Writing a word like JUSTICE in large block letters was relatively easy, Dazzle thought, even when you lacked opposable thumbs. But finding someone who *understood* it—that was a different matter entirely.

Dazzle gazed up at the scraggly-faced man who spent his days driving up and down the main road looking for people to yell at. The man's name was Tom Rodgers.

"Woof," Dazzle said, as clearly as he could. "Woof-woof."

"That's pure horse-shit, little doggy. You need hip-boots to wade through horse-shit that deep."

"Woof," Dazzle continued. Out of the corner of his eye, he noted that the town's strays were beginning to gather in a nearby lot. And Fifi, Mrs. Emerson's poodle, was making her huffy way up Main Street to her daily grooming appointment at All American Pet & Video.

"Woof woof."

"I never said I don't believe in social life, little doggy. I never said I don't respect the basic rights of all creatures—even, when you come down to it, *women.* All I *said* was—"

"Woof," Dazzle said brusquely. He didn't have time for Tom Rodgers today. "Woof."

"And don't give me those crap statistics about accidental gun-fatalities versus deaths by terrorist-attack, or the amount of money we spend every year on AIDs research as opposed to subsidizing the weapons industry. You're just monkeying with the facts, little doggy. You're just trying to confuse me."

"Woof," Dazzle concluded. He didn't even look at Tom Rodgers, whose face had turned sweaty and red. Instead, Dazzle kept his eyes on Fifi, who came prancing neatly his way.

Fifi was aft. Fifi was starboard.

The wink. The pearly smile.

And then she was gone.

While Dazzle's heart reverberated with beauty and light.

"Well, fuck you *too*, little doggy!" Tom Rodgers shouted, flinging a handful of dashboard change at Dazzle's weedy street-corner. "And just you 'member who's beggin' charity from whom, get me? Just 'member who needs it and who gives it, and then you'll know what *justice* means, little doggy! It means *me*! It means your only friend in this lonely world, and he goes by the name of Tom Rodgers!"

As Tom Rodgers stomped off in big black buckled boots, Dazzle gazed across the street at the motley mutts who came from various parts of town to regard him distantly each morning: Elliot, Stouffer, Shauna and Bernard.

"It's amazing how these apish bipeds can get so worked up about their silly opinions," Dazzle opined to his fellow canines, who weren't listening either. "Like anybody in this dirt-locked town gives a rat's ass."

BUT OF COURSE the local dogs had not deigned to speak to Dazzle since his arrival in town nearly three weeks ago. The only words they spoke were to one another.

"He's neither alpha nor beta. That's what knots my socks."

"He neither leads nor follows."

"He just sits there all day with his message board and his bowl of water. Like he's not planning to leave."

"He's got no license, no master, no home to go to. And it doesn't seem to bother him one bit."

"He's got a thing for Fifi, though. Like who doesn't?"

"Give him credit. He doesn't piss on our trees or dig up our bones, and he seems content with whatever pears and figs fall off the local trees. Weird."

"Tried the veggie thing myself a few years back. It's not what it does to your bowels that I find upsetting. It's what it does to your outlook on life."

"Do you think we should try talking to him?"

"What would we say?"

"Like nice ta meetcha. How's it hangin'. That sort of thing."

"He seems more interested in conversing with the townspeople. Maybe he doesn't want to waste his oh-so-valuable time on dogs."

"Doesn't mean we can't be polite."

"If he's got something to say, let him say it."

"I got this old lady on Cherry Street, feeds me scraps every night. Maybe I'll invite him along."

"On Cherry Street. An old lady on Cherry Street."

"Hey. Don't *you* start getting any bright ideas!"

"I KNOW IT'S not *fair*," replied Ariel Sandmeyer, the Chief Clerk at California Federal, who stopped by every morning to present Dazzle the remains of his wife's blueberry pancakes on a white paper napkin. "But that's the way life goes. Do you think it's *fair* for a married man with three kids to be working hourly wages? Do you think it's *fair* to watch my pension swoop up and down the Nasdaq like a wing-struck jet? Some people have it better than other people, and some animals have it better than other animals. It's just the way life's always been."

"Woof," Dazzle said. He always went a bit easy on Ariel. (He blamed it on those damn pancakes). "Woof woof."

"I'm not abdicating my sense of responsibility, guy. I'm just saying–"

"Woof."

"Okay, agreed, just because life's not fair doesn't mean that people shouldn't be. Fairness isn't a condition of the world, granted. It's a *possibility* generated by language-bearing creatures like ourselves."

"Woof."

"And okay, I'll grant you my financial worries are nothing compared to those of homeless mutts. Living on the street and reaping their daily harvest from garbage cans and so forth. But hey, I've got problems, too."

"Woof."

"Yes, it is hard. Especially with kids."

"Woof woof."

"I'll think about it. That's all I promise."

"Woof."

Ariel got up on creaky knees. He took his thin, faded briefcase with him.

"Now really, I gotta go. If I'm late and my boss thinks I've been talking to some homeless dog on the street? He'll put me on Stress-Related leave in two seconds."

IT WAS A dull-as-dishwater town, with very little to provide in the way of Things to Watch. People walked from their cars to the bank and back again, or drove past with truckloads of pumpkins, and rarely did anybody pause long enough to read the words that Dazzle scrawled every day (after much deliberation) on his EZ-Race Message Board, or inquire about what those words might mean.

Equality.
Temerity.
Patience.
Concord.
Endurance.
Peace.

But then Dazzle had never expected the world to beat a path to his door. He only hoped that if he spoke the truth simply enough, somebody might hear.

At sunset, Dazzle usually wandered down to Fifi's and lay his weary bones beside her Capra-esque garden-fence. It was funny, he thought, how he had spent so little time with Fifi, and yet she seemed to be the only bitch in the world who understood what he was about.

"I want you to know that I admire what you're doing," Fifi told him, seated regally in the moonlight like a beautiful porcelain figurine. "Before you came to town, nobody talked about anything but themselves. As in: Guess how many rats I caught last night? Or: Guess how many posts I peed on? But these days, the dogs are finally talking about something other than themselves. They're talking about *you*, Dazzle. They're trying to figure you out."

EVEN THOUGH DAZZLE wasn't what anybody would call modest, Fifi had a way of inspiring his abashedness. He didn't know if he liked this feeling or not.

"Wellll, that's nice of you to say," he would drawl laconically, flinching out an awkward smile. "But I'm not doing this for attention. I'm not trying to make a name for myself, or anything like that."

"I know you're not, Dazzle-honey. But you've done something to this one-horse town, I swear. It use to be that things rolled on because people didn't know any other way of rolling. But now they gotta wonder things they never wondered before. Such as, 'What's Dazzle *really* doing on that stupid street-corner?' Or: 'I wonder what far-flung word he'll come up with next?' And that's the first step, isn't it? Getting people to ask questions. The second step, of course, is getting them to sit down long enough to answer those questions for themselves."

Some nights, Dazzle would lie beside Fifi's fence until almost dawn. Occasionally they even fell asleep together–she on one side of the fence, him on the other.

"I should tell you that I'm practically married," Dazzle whispered once, just before drifting off.

"You already told me, honey."

"I already told you?"

"You made me no promises when you hit town, honey. And I won't make any promises either."

"No promises," Dazzle thought. He was speaking the words to himself as he closed his tired eyes. No promises from me. No promises from you.

"Now get some sleep–you'll need it. Tomorrow's first of the month, and you'll likely be having yourself a steady stream of visitors down there at the bank."

"GOOD MORNING, FELLAH. How's my big doggy?"

"Woof."

"Sorry. I *was* being over-familiar. But I'm excited. I talked your proposals over with the board, and one conversation led to another. I'd like you to meet Al Gullickson."

"Pleased tuh meetcha, doggy."

"Of Gullickson's Custom Decal on Frontage Road."

"We got your Dream Weavers, your Hot & Horny, your Fantasy Leopards, your Stellar Array."

"Woof."

"He's one of the most successful businessmen in the tri-county area and we thought, I mean *I* was thinking, that as bankers we don't just supply capital. We provide interlocutory, information-based services of a highly individualized—"

"Your Desert Storm, your Kabul Peacekeepers, and then plenty of the usual fangoria sluts with Christmas-sized boobs and so forth."

"Woof."

"Well, yes, we *do* do business together. The bank arranges an easily-approved, no-cash-down credit arrangement to both Al and his customers. Customers, I might add, who drive from as far as San Miguel and Pismo for the sort of lifestyle-enhancing mobile-design-craftsmanship they can only find at Gullickson's Custom Decal."

"Our biggest thing this year seems to be Conan the Barbarian battling dragons and his bosom and I mean *bosom*-buddy Red Sonja battling ogres while displaying her huge, I mean these really massive—"

"Woof."

"That's right, fellah. We're here to discuss your idea of a what did you call it?"

"Woof woof."

"A Canine-Outreach Community Center on this abandoned lot here, and everything you said turns out to be true. The lot *does* belong to the city, which can assign deeds for the purpose of community enhancement to interested parties but, well. We just never actually thought of using perfectly decent city-owned property for public services before. It never even crossed our minds."

"I don't even know how you'd battle ogres with a set of armory like that babe's packing I think that's what it's all about, this barbarian thing that won't go away? Guys in bulging loincloths and lady-warriors with these non-terrestrial-sized boobs."

"Woof."

"Yes, he is a little self-obsessed. Most successful people are."

"You can't find Red Sonja-sized boobs anywhere on the planet Earth, that's what I tell my customers. But for a no-down-payment-slash-small-monthly-payment you *can* find her swinging her mighty weaponry on the panel doors of your RV, truck or mini-van. Just come out to Al's Custom Decal, and that's the big howdy two-handed wave I give them, like I'm shouting "Hey, you come on out here!" You've probably seen my all-night movies on Channel thirty-six."

"Woof."

"He doesn't watch TV."

"I'm not deaf, Sandmeyer."

"Woof woof woof."

"Nobody said this Canine-Outreach Center was about promoting Al's Custom Decal, I just thought—"

"Woof."

"No, what I'm saying is that Al provides the start-up capital, and we grant him rights to a small concessions stand and a modest, just the normal-sized—"

"I was thinking an illuminated billboard maybe."

"Or a tastefully-designed, I guess, billboard which, you know, lets people know these public-services have been made possible by—"

"Woof."

"I don't think you're being entirely fair, big fellah."

"Woof-woof."

"I'm sure you *could* accomplish a lot through public-donations, local volunteers and the general good faith of humans and dogs. But it's gonna cost *something*."

"Woof."

"Well, the playground, for one thing."

"Woof."

"For the kids. Monkey bars, slides, spider-net, you know. You can't have a park without—"

"Woof woof."

"Now you *are* being unreasonable."

"And then maybe we could move on to other festivals and so forth. Like Be a Barbarian Day, where everybody dresses up like barbarians and drives here in their RVs, trucks or mini-vans and stage big sword fights and whatnot."

"Woof woof."

"I thought dogs liked kids."

"Woof."

"Well, I guess that is what you might call an 'unexamined assumption'."

"Then maybe King Arthur Day, or Kabul Peacekeepers Day, or Jedi Day, or what else? What kind of festival can you have where the girls might wear those big metal buckets on their–"

"Woof woof."

"I know it seems like a compromise. But that's how you get things done in the real world."

"Woof."

"Okay, *my* real world. That's how you get things done in *my* real world."

"Lady Vampire Day, Lady Amazon Day, Lady Valkyrie Day. I feel like a popcorn machine. The ideas just keep, like, they keep spontaneously erupting in my head."

"Woof," Dazzle said solidly, lay down on the hot pavement, and closed his eyes. He was an island in the middle of a stormy sea, sufficient with its own natural flora and fauna. You could rage at this island for thousands of years and it would always be there, shining in the sun. "Woof woof."

"Just *think* about it, big fellah," Ariel Sandmeyer said sadly, as if he were viewing that island through the wrong end of a telescope. "I'm doing my best to help within the available parameters, okay? Let's not give up on each other yet."

"HE TURNED THEM down."

"No way."

"I was sitting right here. No no no, he said. And the most important human at the bank? All he kept saying was please please please."

"Of all the goddamn nerve."

"Who elected him doggy-Pope?"

"You get these radical-extremists and they don't care for nothing but themselves."

"Free dog food, free dog-beds, a place for taking

dumps and leaving them."

"Maybe even gas-central heating someday. A little cheese-shop, food stamps. An open vet's clinic on Fridays."

"He turned down *our* Community Center?"

"Without even asking our opinion."

"Well burn my butt."

"He comes into town from nowhere. He sits on our freaking curb day after day. He makes eyes at our Fifi and eats scraps from our fruit trees. Declares himself our public spokesperson when. You know. We're perfectly capable of speaking for ourselves."

"Darn tooting."

A general exclamatory "woof" rose from the pack. It startled them.

"What's he writing on that Magic Board of his?"

"I recognize the first letter. What *is* that first letter?"

"Is it... the pointy letter?"

"That's it! The pointy letter. I just wish they made reading glasses for dogs. I could spell out that Message Board no problem."

"There's the pointy letter and it's followed by. The ball. The ball on the stick. The *small* stick!"

Consumed by their own general clamor, the doggish riff-raff grew aware of something moving in their direction. They smelled it before they heard it. It was almost here.

The click-click-click of Fifi's perfectly manicured toes on the pavement as she was escorted home on her leash.

"What the sign *says*," Fifi told them, smiling her bright flash in the dusty street, "is *Start Well/Finish Better*. You boys know what those words mean?"

The dogs shuffled uneasily.

"It means take your best swing coming out of the box, and don't wait for someone else to do what you can do better. 'Cause when it comes to support from your fellow dogs? They'll sell you out before you even reach the plate."

Fifi didn't pause to sniff or piss. She just carried on with the faceless rhythm of her irreproachable master and disappeared down the street.

YOU COULDN'T JUST say no to banking and commerce without stirring up (at the very least) a war of words. And a war of words was precisely what Dazzle was hoping for.

"Good afternoon, you sweet little poochie-dog you. Suzy Robertson from Tri-County Six O'Clock News."

"Woof. Woof woof."

"Yes, well, I guess if an overturned tanker-truck or basement electrical fire proved of concern to our viewers then yes, we'd be there. But that's not *all* we cover. Not by a long shot."

"Woof."

"How about if *I* ask the questions and *you*—"

"Woof woof."

"I don't think that's any of your—"

"Woof."

"My uncle, I guess. He's board member of the bank, and a principal investor in Gullickson's Custom Decal. But what I want to ask is how long you plan to maintain your street-front protest against, what's it say on your EZ-Race Board? Animal Greed and Corruption?"

"Woof."

"You're in no position to insult me *or* my credentials."

"Woof."

"Two years at Los Angeles City College, if you must know. So like how many years did *you* do?"

"Woof."

"Bob, we're not getting anywhere with this mutt. Let's take our cameras across the street for some collateral response."

"Woof."

"Same to you, *sweetie.*"

Dazzle was relieved to watch them drag their cables and lighting equipment towards a different venue of misrepresentation entirely. He still had a few simple things to say, and he didn't want these trauma-merchants screwing it up prime-time.

"Hey there, poochie-dogs. Suzy Robertson from Tri-County Six O'Clock News."

"Rough!" "Grrr!" "Yowp!"

"So then our shaggy friend *doesn't* speak for the community at large."

"Rough!" "Grr!" "Yowp!"

"And basically you're all grateful for the offer of a Canine Refuge and Community Center, as proposed by the bank's board of directors and Gullickson's Custom Decal, one of the Tri-County's most successful home-grown businesses for the past seventeen years."

"Rough!" "Grr!" "Yowp!"

"Yes, he may be a little crazy and even fanatical."

"Rough!" "Grr!" "Yowp!"

"And once the bulldozers arrive it won't matter what one dog thinks, or how selfish he is. All that matters is how soon the Al Gullickson Wildlife

Refuge–"

"Rough!" "Grr!" "Yowp!"

"The *Canine* Wildlife Refuge and Community Center can be made fully operational, bringing good value and discount family savings–"

"Rough!" "Grr!" "Yowp!"

"Well of course it'll cost *some*thing to get in. Perhaps on an ability-to-pay basis, I'm sure that's being considered. *Some*body's paying in the long run so it might as well be the individuals who use it."

"Rough!" "Grr!" "Yowp!"

"Bob? Let's cut here. We've got all we need from these characters."

Dazzle's smile resembled a grimace as he gazed up from his fetal curl. There was one thing you could always count on from the Powers That Be.

They never stopped talking until they told you exactly who they really were.

THAT NIGHT DAZZLE lay on his street-corner and awaited the bulldozers with a sober equanimity. You can't stand your ground until somebody tries to take it away, he reflected dryly. And until somebody tries to take it away, you can never be certain whether it's worth keeping or not.

"You don't have to stare too hard to see that the world's a total mess," Dazzle whispered sadly to Fifi, who had dug a tunnel underneath the white picket fence to reach his beleaguered side. "The demonization of the poor, the outcast, the deluded, the lost. The proliferation of firearms, teletexting, bad media, cell phones, all-talk radio and, I still can't believe they give a degree in it at big-shot universities, but something called media studies, like they're parsing old Benson & Hedges commercials, I kid you not. From what I see, it is now possible to say absolutely nothing to practically the entire planet, and replay it infinitely on your own web-page, since everybody's got a web-page these days and they're all about the same goddamn thing. Nothing. And mark my words, Fifi. As soon as they start turning a profit from our Outreach Center, it'll mean nothing, too. It'll just be another mindless purveyor of fatty burgers, candy-cane, and ice cream. They'll use it to stage political fund-raisers and RV shows and Boat-O-Ramas, and that's something this country really needs, isn't it? More people turning a profit from the basic, unremarkable desire of animals to lie down on the green grass and escape the traffic for a while. Not, 'Hey, how's it feel? Are you comfortable? Can I lie down with you and rest awhile?' But only: 'How much is it worth? You got a valid ticket and I.D.? How 'bout a Jumbo bag of candy-coated popcorn to go with that Slurpee?'"

Fifi and Dazzle weren't spooning to keep warm—it just came naturally. She fit into the crescent of Dazzle's saggy, unexercised belly like a muffin in a corrugated paper sleeve.

"Most animals don't know what they want," Fifi whispered gently. "Which is why they're so eager to swallow whatever somebody else *says* they want. Now let's just enjoy the evening for what it is, honey, and tomorrow? We'll go somewhere different. We'll dream some other dream."

SINCE THERE WAS nothing left for Dazzle to do, he slept soundly until well past midnight when a peculiar form of redemption arrived in the thoroughly unpredictable guise of a '67 Chevy flatbed with rusty mags and bad suspension.

"I hate *anybody* telling me what to do," Tom Rodgers complained as he unloaded shovels, rakes and sacks of musty peat. "I hate when the government does it, or the courts do it, or the tax people do it. I even hate when the librarian tells me I've got an overdue book, that evil old bitch. And while I may also hate being told what to do by a mangy mutt with an EZ-Race message board, I hate being told what to do by the cops, the mayor, the bank, and the bulldozers even more. All my life, little doggy, people been telling me I'm too angry. My Mommy, my Daddy, my ex-wife, even my kids. But when it comes to getting things done, there are times when anger's all you need. Everything else just gets in the way."

Before he knew what was happening or why, Dazzle found himself digging sleepily at the hard, encrusted dirt with his forepaws. It had been years since Dazzle had stooped so low as to bury a bone in the yard, let alone to perform manual labor, but this felt good from the start. Just doing what came naturally.

"The face of goodness," Fifi said beside him, helping dislodge a broken cinder block, "is often just as bland and unsurprising as the face of evil. Didn't you say that once, honey?"

Dazzle watched Tom Rodgers swing bundled saplings and bushes from the back of his truck with a graceless, edgy intrepidity. It was almost like malice.

"No, sweetheart. But watching our new friend, Tom Rodgers, working his butt off to save our project? I sure wish I had."

WHEN THE BULLDOZERS and local news crews arrived the next morning, they found Dazzle and his companions sleeping peacefully on a quarter-acre of freshly-laid green sod, shaded by several potted maples, willows and oak trees. As it turned out, Tom Rodgers had been developing a pretty substantial botanical preserve out there on his bankrupt mink-ranch, and he didn't mind sharing the excess. "I figured it all might prove useful someday in one of my life-long career-ambitions. Which, as most people round here know, is to become either the world's best-equipped survivalist, or a trip-wire vet."

"**Please remove yourselves from the occupied zone**!" commanded Officer Ramdale through a sleek, emergency-coded red and yellow bullhorn. "**You are obstructing the development of municipal property! If you do not voluntarily remove yourselves from the property, you will be forcibly removed! The choice is yours!**"

"Bite me," Dazzle said, without looking up.

"**What's that? What did you say, old soldier?**"

"He said *woof!*" barked Tom Rodgers. "What's the matter with you, Paul? Are you deaf?"

"**Now that's enough from you, Tom. I'm only trying to do my—**"

"Okay now, Paul," Ariel Sandmeyer interposed, and stepped forward to flick off the bullhorn switch. "Everybody can hear you just fine."

Officer Ramdale blinked twice, as if awakening from a dream of watching himself on TV. Then he looked around at the street-corner crowd, which consisted of the local postman, a trucker named Dave Kobis, a near-indigent fry-cook, and a pair of

Japanese tourists, happily snapping photos of what had to be the most annoying mutt on the entire planet.

The bulldozer operators, poised atop their respective machinery, squinted at the sun and smoked their morning butts.

"Someone was busy last night," Ariel Sandmeyer said, testing the verge of green grass with the toe of his soft-leather shoe.

Tom Rodgers stepped forward. He was wearing the same dirt-stained Wranglers and white denim shirt he had worn since his senior year in high school nearly three decades before.

"Non-profit," Tom said.

Ariel continued stroking the green grass seductively with his tan penny-loafer.

"We could, you know. We could live with that."

"Post no bills."

"We might be able to restrict said bills from being posted."

"People, and of course dogs, can lie on this grass anytime they want. They can come from anywhere they happen to come from. And just because the cops don't know them, right. That don't make them criminals."

"Woof," Dazzle interjected.

"And it don't make them strays, neither."

The crowd's attention was starting to turn in the direction of Ariel Sandmeyer and Officer Ramdale. Even a few of the town's grumpiest, most xenophobic mutts were wandering over to join Dazzle and Fifi on the warm grass.

Elliot and Stouffer. But not Bernard.

They didn't look at Dazzle, though. And Dazzle

didn't look at them.

Try appealing to a dog's mind, Dazzle thought, and prepare for disappointment. But try appealing to their sorry butts and that's a different story.

For the first time that morning, Ariel smiled.

"Of course I can't speak for Officer Ramdale and the Parkridge Police Department," he told Tom Rodgers. "But I'll see what we can do."

BY THE TIME Dazzle left town, he had almost learned to accept the children's playground, the children's water fountain, the children's picnic area and, worst of all, the children, who arrived in a shrieking motley lather every afternoon when the schools let out at three-thirty.

"You've got to make compromises if you want to get things done," he shrugged philosophically. "And so long as they keep the brats on their side of the fence, I don't think they do any harm."

Dazzle was saying goodbye to Fifi on the same street-corner where they had met, slept, dreamed and triumphed together. Looking back now and feeling sentimental, Dazzle thought that the best part was the sleeping. Not-knowing and not-being all at once. But doing it together.

"Well, you know where to find me, honey," Fifi flirted modestly. She was a stiff-upper-lip sort of girl.

They were standing underneath a wood-burned sign that marked the front entrance to the All-Canine Freedom Preserve: a bowling-lane sized strip of grass with open access, shady trees, and a perpetually running, bowl-shaped fountain. The water tasted slightly alkaline. Dazzle could live with that, too.

It wouldn't matter, but he said it anyway.

"You could always come along. There's plenty of room, and I'm sure the other dogs wouldn't mind."

Dazzle gestured with his nose at his old friend Grunt, who was standing down the street in an attitude of general keenness–his senses thrumming with the sky, the clouds, the bugs, the *everything*.

That goddamn Grunt, Dazzle sighed.

Fifi didn't look down the road, or at anything in the world that wasn't Dazzle. "And where would I do my hair, honey? Or my nails? And after a few weeks without my deodorizers, well, excuse me for saying, sweetie. But I'd start smelling as bad as *you*."

Dazzle was gazing reflectively at his fellow dogs, who lay in clumpy accord upon the shady grass with all the self-determination they could muster. As they slept, their tails flicked involuntarily at flies, and their half-lidded eyes twitched out the inner logic of dreams.

"They don't always know what they want or how to get it," Fifi said, with a trace of admiration. "But they appreciate what they've got, and that's what I love about them. It makes them different from you or me."

Feeling for the first time in his life like Gary Cooper, Dazzle licked her face. It was finally time to go.

"When your pals wake up, tell them something for me, will you?"

"I already know what you're going to say. Isn't that funny? Like we're on the same wave-length or something."

Trotting briskly up the street to meet Grunt, who sat waiting at a fork in the road, Dazzle called back over his shoulder:

"Woof," without irony or inflection. "Tell everybody that, before I left town, I told them all, 'Woof.'

5. DAZZLE THE PUNDIT

FOR A LATE middle-aged mutt with barely three weeks of obedience school under his collar, Dazzle was as surprised as anybody to be awarded a Seymour Fischer Guest Professorship from the Free University in Berlin.

"As awkward as it is to admit, Herr Dazzle, you were not exactly our first choice," confessed Dr. Krantzbaum on the day he called to arrange the opening address. "But you would be surprised by how difficult it is to find a decent lecturer in Post-Humanist Studies, especially these days. When Oscar the Baboon canceled at the last minute, we found ourselves grasping at straws. We contacted internationally-renown cats, songbirds, dancing bears, penguins, gender-neutral pachyderms, and even a high-profile crow we once heard about, but they were all booked into the next decade. Then, just as we were about to give up hope, someone told us about you–and your history of iron-jawed protest against the forces of sapien-hegemony and control. And the movie deal, *mein Gott*, that really perked our ears. Be straight with us, Herr Dazzle. Is it true about Sean Penn playing the lead in your life story? If he's not too busy, perhaps you might even arrange a guest appearance for your class."

While Dazzle had been giving the matter serious consideration for the last two weeks or so, he hadn't come close to making a decision until he heard Dr Krantzbaum's strong, sensible voice reaching out for him through the speaker phone.

"I'm genuinely tempted," Dazzle said, sitting at his lawyer's desk in a large leather-bound swivel chair. "I really am. I've always wanted to visit foreign countries and learn about different cultures and so forth, and goodness knows I'm not getting any younger. But frankly, the idea of presenting a public lecture makes me queasy, and while I've always possessed the gift of gab, I might start feeling pretty intimidated if, you know. People actually started *listening*. What I'm trying to say is that I'd hate to be a big disappointment to you guys. Especially since you'd be putting me up in that nice apartment off the Rüdesheimer Platz, and paying me such a hefty per diem and all."

The transatlantic connection was as crisp and clear as a cold glass of water.

"Ach, don't worry about it, old boy! How could our students be disappointed by a big friendly doggy like yourself? We are big dog lovers here in Berlin, Herr Dazzle. We love big shaggy doggies very much."

Dazzle was sitting alone in his lawyer's office, gazing up at shelves of tightly-bound legal volumes which likewise seemed to be gazing down at him. You make a few bucks, Dazzle reflected, sell a few pieces of yourself, and pretty soon it gets harder and harder to escape back into the woods for any decent length of time. There's always another contract to sign, or another call to take.

"Herr Dazzle? Are you still there?"

But then some pieces of yourself are easier to sell than others.

"Yes, Doctor Krantzbaum, and one more thing. As embarrassing as it is to admit, you should know that I don't speak a word of German. This might prove a problem, considering I'm supposed to be giving lectures and all."

The speaker phone breathed a long, happy sigh.

"*Ach, mein doggy freunde!* Bother yourself no longer about this minor difficulty. Our students are very knowledgeable and hard-working, and their canine is quite excellent, as you will soon find out. Many of them, in fact, speak it even better than myself!"

DAZZLE'S RECEPTION WAS held in the lecture hall of the Department of Comparative Cultures, a low-ceilinged, aluminum-sided, mobile-home-like structure set among many fragrant bushes and trees.

"You should know right off that I'm not a trained scholar. Heck, when I was a pup? I barely learned how to roll over and play dead, which led to some pretty uncomfortable confrontations with my first (and only) human family, the Davenports. No, I'm what you'd call an autodidactic sort of dog, which is probably what makes me so skeptical about authority figures and so forth. Political leaders, say. Or movies, newspapers, the world-wide-web and, well, I hope this doesn't sound rude, but even highbrow academic-types such as yourselves. I simply don't believe anything I can't see, hear, taste and sniff for my goddamn self. It's not that I think I'm better than anybody else. It's just that I never met anybody who's any better than me–if you can dig the distinction."

They were probably the best-looking group of human beings Dazzle had ever seen in his life: well dressed, well fed, and attentive. But it didn't seem right somehow. All these attractive young people sitting politely in hard foldable chairs and wasting their formidable concentration on *him*.

"I guess what I'm saying is that I believe in honest advertising, and to be totally honest? I probably don't have anything interesting to teach you guys except, of course, what it's like to be a dog in a human world. So I hope I won't be too boring, or distract you from the very useful work you're probably doing in your other classes. And, well, at this point I should probably ask if there are any questions. And if there aren't any questions, I can let you all go home."

Dazzle was already climbing down from his awkward perch on the rim of a rickety pine table when he saw a hand go up. The young woman attached to that hand was so beautiful and well-formed that she could put a dog off other dogs.

"I am Agatha Meineke, Herr Professor Dazzle, and I was wondering–"

"Please. Just Dazzle."

She blushed. "If you don't mind my asking, what happens to dogs in America when they refuse to roll over and play dead?"

Her yips and arfs, despite a weird inflection, were almost perfect.

"Nobody feeds them," Dazzle explained simply. "Nobody loves them. They get sent to extermination camps. And if they manage to dig their way out under the fence, they spend the rest of their lives on the lam, running from one garbage can to another. If they're lucky, like me, they might make a nice life for themselves in the woods. But most of them aren't lucky. They get picked up by the Man. They get run over by cars."

Three more hands went up. Four. Five.

"Are you sure you are providing an accurate representation of canine life in America?" enquired a young man with a spiny Norwegian burr. "Many of us receive a different impression entirely from your highly entertaining television programs, in which dogs are profound and witty creatures adored by everyone. Billionaires leave them mansions in their will. They live like kings and queens in the lap of luxury."

It was almost sweet, Dazzle thought. Some Norwegian kid believing what he saw on American TV.

Television," Dazzle replied simply, "only imagines what can't be believed. Otherwise, why would there be so many freaking commercials?"

"Are you claiming that in the Land of Liberty, freedom does not exist for everyone?"

"Only if you can afford it."

A buzz of reflected glances and whispers. Then, from the back of the room, another hand went up.

And signaled that the buzz was over.

"Yes. You in back."

The audience emitted a long, collective sigh. A few even rolled their eyes.

"Heinrich Mandelbrot," the young man said. He wore black from head to foot: black turtleneck, black jeans, black loafers. "Abstract philosophy."

"How's it hanging, Heinrich."

Heinrich leveled his pupil-filled gaze at Dazzle, as

if aiming a rifle.

"When you label yourself an empiricist, are you referring to empiricism of the logical or moral variety? And wouldn't you say that contemporary research into the combinatory nature of public perception has proven conclusively–"

"Oh jeez, Heinrich. I don't think I can answer this."

"Please let me finish. How can you believe what you learn for yourself when you lack the intellectual, moral, or political grounds for knowing who you are to begin with? I'm speaking in a meta-linguistic framework, of course."

"Oh," Dazzle said with a slow, wise nod of his head. He felt a little woozy and out of breath. "The meta-linguistic thingy. Like how do I know I exist outside my head, or something like that?"

The entire audience subsided, as if all the air were being let out of their tires.

"No, Herr Dazzle, I am merely seeking a critical self-appraisal in terms of post-Descartian discourse. I'm sure you're familiar with Habermas. I'm sure you're familiar with the Frankfurt School of Social Research."

Now Dazzle wasn't entirely unfamiliar with post-war German philosophy. As a pup, he had browsed vigorously through many books that fell in his path, and had even snuck off to a college lecture or two. But it all seemed so terribly far away, he thought now. And the idea of those well-meaning German exiles wandering the sun-struck streets of Santa Monica just made him feel lonely.

Sometimes, he thought, it's not *what* you say that matters. It's simply making the effort to say anything at the exact same moment when someone's ready to listen.

"Excuse me, Heinrich. I'm not what you'd call a systematic thinker, but perhaps I can answer your question. But only with another question."

It was like snapping on all the lights in a dark room—causing the audience of really attractive people to look up with an expression that Dazzle didn't often find in the faces of human beings.

Hope?

"And that question is this: don't you think it's time you and your pals led me to some of this Weissbier and sauerkraut I've heard so much about? We've got all term to discuss epistemology, but after traveling fifteen hours baggage class in the bowels of a jumbo jet—hey. This little doggy is *starved*."

FROM THAT DAY forward, Dazzle liked to say that he had Berliners eating out of his hand. But then, nobody enjoyed an inverted metaphor more than Dazzle.

"When I saw my first canine dumping ground at the Tiergarten," Dazzle told his class during one of his typically aimless, unprepared lectures, "I couldn't believe my eyes. Unlike those dead spaces you find in the States, it wasn't carpeted over with broken bottles, hypodermics and whatnot, or located in the worst part of town. It actually had flowerbeds, and a little doggy water fountain, it was classic. I'm not saying you guys got it perfect here in Berlin; that's not what I'm saying at all. But compared to the States, you still have this fairly workable notion of public life. Public parks, public playgrounds, public transport, even socialized medicine—and it works. Whoever woulda thunk it?"

Dazzle realized that his lectures probably didn't qualify as "educational". He was simply gabbing aimlessly about whatever struck his fancy. Yet students were always thanking him for his time and patience; the prettier girls openly scratched him behind the ears and cooed sweet endearments ("What a nice big doggy!") even during office hours with the door open; and meals at the University cafeteria were surprisingly tasty–though nobody in this far-flung and not-quite-fallen empire seemed to realize that there was such a thing as green vegetables.

It was only Heinrich, really, who reminded Dazzle that he wasn't measuring up to his role as intellectual mentor. At times, he even made him feel guilty about it.

"Herr Professor Dazzle! One moment of your time!"

"Please, just Dazzle. Or poochie-dog. Everybody in the States thinks they can call me poochie-dog–you might as well call me poochie-dog too."

"I'm so sorry, Herr Professor, but I was thinking about our discussion yesterday and I still don't understand. Let us imagine, as we were saying, that your doggy consciousness is a goldfish in a goldfish bowl. Is that acceptable?"

"Sure, Heinrich; whatever. But I have this problem with abstract speculation, see. Ideas about ideas about, you know, ideas."

"Now inside this goldfish bowl, everything feels cozy. Your gravel, your ceramic castle, your bubbling air filter, even your benignly puckered reflection in the mineral-streaked glass."

"I think I follow, Heinrich. Nothing but goldfish

bowl. So far as the eye can see."

"But beyond this glass, everything is different. Space, weight, distance. It's inhabited by huge, distorted creatures. Sometimes they notice you; but most of the time, they don't."

"We're not talking ontology, are we, Heinrich? Not about knowing the world, or its reality. But simple communication, right? You speaking to me; and me speaking to you."

"There is a quite fascinating story about Goethe and Schiller, who were discussing, if I remember correctly, the difference between experience and ideas–"

"Goethe and Schiller," Dazzle said slowly. He could see the thronging crowds of the Metro station just ahead. Middle-aged men and women in muted primary colors; college kids in backpacks and denim. He felt himself hurrying towards them. "As much as I'm enjoying our little discussion, Heinrich, I'm afraid this is where I get off."

"*Formbewusstein*," Heinrich enunciated harshly. "Surely not an unfamiliar concept for you, Herr Professor. You being such an internationally-renown intellectual and all."

"Form-buh-whatsit," Dazzle muttered thickly. These Germans sure like ideas, he thought. "Meet me in my office just before class and I promise. This time I won't be late like, you know. The last couple times."

It was just about the only lie Dazzle had told anybody in years. And the funny part was? It didn't bother him at all.

"THE SAD FACT of the matter," Doctor Krantzbaum explained over a friendly, inter-collegiate lunch at Café Einstein, "is that nobody wants to swim in the goldfish bowl with poor Heinrich. He is simply too much *Sturm und Drang*, even for us Germans. He is too much *dasein-en-sich* and *fur-en-sich*, too much *unterheimlich*, too much *shadenfreude*, too much *weltanschauung* and definitely, definitely too much Wagner. Perhaps you have not noticed, Mein Doggy, but our new Germany is a far more lighthearted and unassuming place than it once was. We have taken the lead in the common market, and opened our collective hearts to Super Mario and American Pie. We have even adopted many hip expressions from you laid-back California-types, such as 'go with the flow,' 'tell me about it,' and 'let's get it on.' If I were to boil this cultural sea-change down to a simple analogy: today's Germany is a lot less Goethe and a lot more *Friends*. You know, as in that weekly assembly of footloose, wacky, and perpetually inter-pollinating youths who enliven our otherwise drab television programs many nights of the week." Dr Krantzbaum leaned back and gazed at the bright, chandeliered ceiling, his voice suddenly hushed and reverent. "Now *that's* what I call a proper Isolde, Mein Doggy. The sloe-eyed, sharp-tongued one who stole Brad Pitt's heart a few years ago. She is definitely the unattainable fulfillment of all my trans-celestial yearnings."

Dazzle liked the Café Einstein, where they kept the long-stemmed glasses filled with fruity red wine. He liked the shiny white linen tablecloths, the gilded mirrors, the pervasive whiff of coarse-ground sausage, and the multiply-reflected images of very old men accompanied by youngish, dyed-blonde second wives wearing too much jewelry.

"I'm not saying that I dislike Heinrich," Dazzle explained distantly, scanning the wide hand-written menu with barely-concealed bemusement. (Pork venison beef beef lamb pork pork chicken and fish.) "But he does make me feel like a charlatan. Here he is, coming to class every day with so many intense, well prepared questions about the truth of perception, and the meaning of reality, and here I am, supposed to be his teacher, and I don't have a thing to tell him. I look at Heinrich, I look at the clock on the wall, and I simply don't know how to shut him up. Like just yesterday—what was old Heinrich on about yesterday? Something about nature's excess of sensation. According to Heinrich, nature pulses with so much raw experiential stuff that our meager animal senses can't possibly take it all on board. Heinrich calls it a 'reality-deficit disorder,' and according to Heinrich, this is why our lives continually reverberate with insufficiency and loss."

Dr Krantzbaum was already brooding into the final sips of his Black Forest Bergundy. For one long moment, Dazzle thought the good doctor might be getting as tired of Dazzle as Dazzle was getting of Heinrich.

Finally, Doctor Krantzbaum replied softly: "Insufficiency, yes, in the face of all our Isoldes. And now, if you do not mind, I will place my order for the pork roast and mashed potatoes with gravy, and thus distract myself from that smug grin I see before me always on that barbarian, you know. That movie star who goes by the name of Brad Pitt."

ACCORDING TO HERR Doctor Krantzbaum, Heinrich's peasant-stock Mom, a vender of home-made pottery in Tabruk, had been engaged (non-matrimonially-speaking) by Heinrich's errant Bavarian father enroute to an international hang-gliding competition on the Greek Isles, where he promptly soared from the rocky cliffs like Icarus and fell just as hard. As a result, Heinrich grew up envisioning Germany as more than a metaphoric and always-absent Fatherland; it was the fulfillment of identity towards which his overhuge heart always yearned. He grew up reading German poetry, listening to German opera on his Walkman, reading German culture pages, and replaying Fassbinder on his video until he knew every halting line of dialog and every swooping camera-fugue by heart. Eventually, he attended German schools on a DAAD fellowship, and during his third year at his dead papa's alma mater in Cologne, produced a highly-regarded honor's thesis, entitled *Hegel, Kant, Marx and Adorno: When is Too Much Not Enough?* that won him a State Arts Grant to Frankfurt, where he completed his baccalaureate at seventeen on the subject of Ossian. Since his arrival at FU, however, he had yet to complete a single chapter of his dissertation. But this had not prevented him from mapping out so many ambitious lifetime projects that it made his advisor's head hurt.

"I am compiling notes for a trilogy on the failure of knowledge," Heinrich breathlessly explained on their long afternoon walks to the Metro, while Dazzle just as breathlessly tried to outdistance him. "Then there is my history of Prussian Absolutism, my critique of Benjamin's radical desubjectivization of spirit, an essay on the anxiety of essay-writing and, of course, my reschematization of German philosophy since Lessing, which should encompass at least twenty book-length manuscripts and lead me to the doorstep of my self-proposed life-time project: to chart the intellectual DNA of God through the prose and poetry of every heterotext on the Internet. What do you think about that for a lifetime project, Herr Dazzle? I realize it may sound excessively ambitious, but as you must know by now—if there's one thing I'm not afraid of, it's excess."

Walking with Heinrich was like trying to win a race with your own obsessions. No matter how fast you thought you were going, they were always a few steps ahead of you already—even on two feet.

"Don't you ever get lonely, Heinrich?" Dazzle asked one day when they found themselves slumped side-by-side on a leafy, convenient bus bench just short of the Metro. "Don't you ever feel that you're spending too many nights alone in your bed?"

"German women are afraid of making commitments," Heinrich replied sulkily, nostrils flaring. "Especially when it comes to making commitments with Heinrich."

"What about TV or movies, Heinrich? Or even Nintendo? Just something, you know, to get your mind off itself."

"German TV is nothing but bourgeois propaganda about the terrible, nonsensical traumas associated with being bourgeois. And as for American TV, forget it. Dreams of plenitude, twenty four hours a day. And as you must realize, Herr Dazzle—those aren't the sort of dreams that fool me at all."

"Then what about a good cause, Heinrich? Like working with kids, or cleaning up the environment? You can't spend your entire life being obsessed with *Liebestod*, Heinrich. Especially when you have so much trouble just getting a date."

"Heinrich has no trouble getting dates."

"Okay, second dates."

"Making love is the death of desire."

"But it clears the head, Heinrich. It keeps you from thinking too hard about things you can't change. Like, you know. Yourself."

"Heinrich refuses to turn his back on the universe which today's Germany does not wish to acknowledge. The universe of heartache, spiritual insufficiency and loss."

"Tristan and Isolde."

"Who told you about Tristan and Isolde?"

"I may be a dog, Heinrich," Dazzle explained with a sigh. "But *everybody's* heard of Tristan and Isolde."

WHEN IT CAME to unraveling the complex knot of human nature, Dazzle had limited means at his disposal. But sometimes you have to make the effort, he thought. Even when you have no idea what's going on.

"Heinrich is perfectly attractive," conceded Agatha on the afternoon Dazzle asked her into his office for an informal chat. "And he certainly boasts the sort of passionate intelligence that a girl doesn't often come across in our new, improved Germany. But at the same time, he's a really tough date, especially with all his engines running. After an endless bus ride during which he continuously talks about Hegel, you end up at some badly lit cafeteria, where the rubber-gloved staff clearly find him offensive. And every time you try to change the subject to something interesting—such as your long-unconfessed ambitions to win the Euro-Vision Song Contest, or the latest episode of

Friends–he just scowls terribly, as if you have hurled hot pasta in his face. He begins spouting Nietzsche or Hölderlin, and raving about the mindless herds of contemporary culture. Pretty soon it's nothing but 'bourgeoisie-this' and 'bourgeoisie-that,' and he's not even looking at you anymore, or noticing how much trouble you went to with your hair. Once, I was so upset, I started crying into my bratwurst. And did he notice? No, he didn't notice at all. But in answer to your question, I could actually imagine sleeping with Heinrich, or even accompanying him in a romantic manner to your highly-publicized lecture at the Cross-Humanities Institute next week. But I'm afraid I can't imagine doing these things until he learns how to shut his stupid mouth for more than two seconds."

Agatha was sitting with Dazzle in his office on the swaybacked, well-worn sofa, and aimlessly scratching his rump while she talked. Dazzle realized that this was probably not the sort of situation a professor should cultivate with his most attractive female student (even if it was Europe). But then, what the hey, he thought. It helped him think.

"So what you're saying, Agatha, is that you want to be with Heinrich. But only if he stops telling you who he really is."

Agatha considered this for a moment.

"I guess that's what I *am* saying, Herr Dazzle. Does that sound superficial?"

Dazzle almost laughed.

"No, Agatha, I don't think it does. Especially when we're talking about Heinrich."

Which was when Dazzle realized that he might have something to teach his students after all.

"I THINK I resemble the funny, wacky, sometimes stupid-sounding one named Joey. Don't I seem like Joey to you, Herr Doktor? I certainly feel like Joey— now that I'm getting to know him, that is."

It was amazing, Dazzle thought, how quickly these European types could pick up a totally new language. It was like dealing with chameleons or something.

"Well, yeah, I guess so, Heinrich. Joey, right. And his hair's always slightly disarranged in a kind of attractive fashion. Just like yours."

Heinrich pulled vainly at his crumpled locks. "And he always looks so baffled when he learns something obvious that everybody else has known all along. Like one of the other friends feels inclined towards him physically. Or two of his fellow friends are having an affair. He is very naive and easily astounded. Much like I feel myself to be almost all of the time."

"Boyish vulnerability," Dazzle added, trying to help. "And innocence. Don't forget innocence, Heinrich."

They had just finished screening the first three seasons in the audio-visual Common Room, where Dazzle was enjoying his best attendance of the term. The chairs and tables were full, and many students were sitting cross-legged on the linoleum.

"Myself," piped up Ingrid, a beautiful, fair-skinned Swiss woman who hadn't uttered a single word before now, "I must confess strong feelings of similarity to the very sarcastic one with the blonde hair, though my own hair is far too curly and boring. I often aim my wicked barbs at people for no reason whatsoever, and many do not appreciate my characteristically bizarre sense of humor."

Hands were being raised by students Dazzle had

never seen before. Some of them weren't even listed on his register.

"We especially enjoy their manifest looks of surprise when they awaken in each other's beds. And no matter what sort of insurmountable problems they face–such as achieving personal space in their bathrooms, or the ominous threat of really attractive non-friends trying to break into the inner circle–they still feel total devotion to one another without exception, and raise their variously-engendered (and highly attractive) offspring in total harmony."

"Except perhaps for that English girl. We have trouble accepting that a true friend would ever marry an English girl."

"It was doomed from the start."

"She hardly makes any subsequent appearances."

"She was nowhere near so entertaining as Sean Penn."

"Which brings us to a collective point of interest, Herr Dazzle, if you wouldn't mind–"

After snoozing through the entire DVD marathon, Dazzle had awoken to a class buzzing with excited young men and women learning about one another as fast as they could. Especially Agatha and Heinrich, who were sitting so close together that they almost touched.

Dazzle even felt enough confidence to tackle the most troubling issue of the term:

"I think I know where this is going, so let me reiterate for like the thousandth time. There's nothing to those rumors about Sean Penn playing the lead in my life story. And I hate to disappoint you–but at this point in time? I doubt if Sony will even renew the option."

IT WAS NEVER easy for Dazzle to tell when he had turned a potentially disastrous experience into a marginally successful one, but he was pretty sure the breakthrough occurred sometime during his presentation of the Seymour Fischer Lecture, which was held at the Modern Language Institute, conveniently located just across the street from the Mitte Metro.

"First off," Dazzle began, "I want to tell you all *woof*, and say that I've had a terrific time during the last few months, *woof woof*. And just as expected, I've ended up learning more from you guys than you could ever learn from me, especially when it comes to language. For example, I've learned that you guys really take language seriously, not simply as a means of expressing yourselves (like most American mutts I know), but as a means of communicating with other cultures. You guys actually listen to other people, whatever country they're from. I guess it's the result of living on a continent with so many various languages and all, and everybody competing for the same euros and shelf-space. And so far as your canine—hey, stop apologizing! For my money, you speak it as well as any dog, right down to the guttural dipthongs. Good going!"

The large audience of well-dressed, attractive men and women smiled a collective smile.

(When in doubt, just compliment these people on their language skills, Dazzle thought happily. It's like turning on all the lights.)

"Anyway," Dazzle continued, shouldering up to the low-slung microphone, "I'll never forget my time in your country, or the things I've learned while I was here. For example, I now realize that language isn't just a pile of words in a dictionary. Language is the air we breathe, and the food we eat, and the stories we tell when we're together. Look, I know I can be pretty cynical and footsore about this crazy world, but there's one thing I've learned which gives me hope. Every effort to speak or listen is basically a good effort, so long as we keep trying. Which is, I guess, a long-winded way of saying thanks for having me. I had a terrific time. Oh–and one more thing."

The audience moved forward just a little to the edge of their chairs. Dazzle didn't think he'd ever get use to it: the posture and intensity of almost-alien human beings listening.

To *him*.

(What a trip, Dazzle thought.)

"*Herzlichen   Dank   fuer   Ihre   wunderbare Gastfreundschaft,*" Dazzle enunciated thickly, in possibly the worst German ever spoken on the face of the planet. "And now, if you don't mind, it's time for me to go."

6. DAZZLE JOINS THE SCREENWRITER'S GUILD

DAZZLE FOUND HIS first script conference a lot less painful than he expected.

"I see a dog with severe personality disorders," envisioned Syd Fleishman of Sony Tristar, seated in his overstuffed leather arm-chair with a plastic liter of Evian propped between his knees. "I see a dog with closeness issues, and issues about his dad. I see a dog with lots to say about the terrible problems facing mankind—such as the destruction of the ozone layer and the rainforests, and the tragedy of Native Americans and all that. But I also see a dog that, well. If he spots a human being in trouble? That dog comes running. An all-faithful sort of dog, but an all-faithful sort of dog with *attitude*. You gotta *earn* the respect of a dog like that. But once you earn that respect, he's your buddy for life."

Syd was flanked by the Head of Creative Development and the Vice-Head of Corporate Production. Dazzle couldn't remember the names of either of these high-flying, barely-post-graduate executives, but throughout the entire 45 minute conference nobody let him forget for one second that the CEO's name was Syd.

"It's a bold new animal movie for a bold new millennium, *Syd*," piped-up the Head of Creative Development.

"It's got heart, *Syd*. It's got action. And what's more," interjected the Vice Head of Corporate Production, "it's got abstract topicality. Abstract topicality, see, is this term I kind of invented."

Dazzle was leafing through a telephone-book-sized legal contract. The redacted passages alone were terrifying in their opaqueness.

"Kind of like Capra or Spielberg," continued the Vice Head, even though everybody had already stopped listening. "You know, like stuff that *seems* to be about current affairs? But once you look closely, it's not about anything at all."

This particular lull wasn't on the morning agenda.

"Any questions?" Syd asked, getting to his feet. It was the only appointment that Syd was never late for: lunch.

Dazzle took this opportunity to gesture at the as-yet unsigned contract with a flaky forepaw.

"Look, Syd. I've been reading through this rancid sack of worms, and if you don't mind my asking, I'm still hazy on a couple details."

Syd, frozen in an attitude of benign departure, smiled stiffly.

"What a cute little doggy," whispered the Head of Creative Development. She looked about nineteen years old. "He wants to discuss his contract. He wants to be part of the legal process, too."

Three sets of executive eyes, Dazzle thought. And once they start exchanging ironic, bemused glances, it's impossible to tell them apart.

"As I understand," Dazzle went on, "you guys aren't trying to produce a major motion picture based on my life. Rather you're buying the rights, and I quote, 'to develop a long-running, multi-format entertainment entity based on the [possibly fictive] events and characters inspired by the legally-recognized intellectual-commodity-unit known as Dazzle'. Which leaves me wondering, guys–why so much trouble and expense? Why not just make up your own character and call him, oh, like Harry the dog, or Bozo the cat or something? Then you could 'develop' any damn thing you pleased, and you wouldn't have to pay me anything, or negotiate so many clause-belaboring details with my annoying agent. I may be a dog, guys, but that doesn't make me stupid. All I'm asking is what could I possibly possess that you guys can't invent for yourselves? Give it to me straight, *Syd*. I really want to know."

Syd was smiling at the memory of something he had once said, or a person he use to be. It was a self-enclosed, inviolate sort of smile. He didn't have to share it with anybody.

"That's simple, Daz. You got the only thing money can't buy in this town."

Dazzle waited. So did everybody else.

"Authenticity," Syd said.

And left the building.

ACCORDING TO *THE Who's Who Hollywood Guide to Selling Your First Screenplay*, Fred Prescott had won an Oscar during the Eisenhower administration for his collaborative work on some long-forgotten skirt-and-sandal bio-pic, and his consequent A-list status had carried him through lean years and fat. But his work habits were rudimentary; he lacked even the crudest of social graces; and most mornings, his biggest achievement seemed to be dragging his sorry butt out of bed for black coffee and a cinnamon bagel.

"You can't make a whore of Lady Inspiration," Fred often said. "You can only leave the front door open and hope she stops by for a while. Never sweat art, Daz-baby. That's rule *numero uno* at the House of Fred."

Dazzle, who had never stared into the eyes of a looming contract deadline before, couldn't quite adopt Fred's free and easy manner. He knew it made him sound pro-establishment; he just couldn't help himself.

"I'm not saying we should make a whore of Lady Inspiration, Fred," Dazzle explained in his most laid-back, diplomatic manner. "I'm just saying it's been three weeks, and we don't have a title, or even a two sentence plot summary. Just that rather vague opening scene in the garbage dump with two topless teenagers, which you say is modeled on Italian what?"

"Post-war existential *nouvelle-vague*," Fred said sharply, giving Dazzle a slow once over, like a school guard scanning for concealed weaponry. "Are you saying you've never heard of Antonioni, pooch? What sort of writing partner did they saddle me with, anyway?"

The funniest thing about movie people, Dazzle thought, was that no matter how laid-back they pretended to be, their fuses were always incredibly short. It was as if Dazzle had to apologize constantly for all the things they thought he said.

"I'm not saying I don't like the garbage dump scene, Fred. In fact, I probably like the garbage dump scene a lot. I just don't think it's enough material to deliver to Sony after six weeks work. It might need, you know. A little embellishment."

It was like prodding an open wound.

"So you want to embellish our natural-birth baby, is that it? Like wrap it up in pretty bows and whatnot and shoot fireworks out its ass? Why don't you, a first-timer who struck it lucky, explain the business to me, the Oscar winning sole-credited story-designer of *Solon the Magnificent*, *War Bond Baby*, and the recently rediscovered 'AMC forgotten comedy-classic,' *I Can't Stop Dancing!* Maybe *I* need an introductory scriptwriting lesson from a dickless wonder like yourself."

By this point, the remains of Fred's cinnamon bagel were starting to look pretty tempting, causing Dazzle's tail to thump impatiently at the polished hardwood floor. But then, so did the long blue beach extending beyond the smudgy picture window, and the endless California summer filled with leathery-skinned, once-attractive people playing volleyball and frisbee golf.

In his long and shaggy life, Dazzle had never actually explored Zuma.

But maybe it was high time he did.

DAZZLE WAS USUALLY returning from his second or third walk of the morning when it came time to pay that morning's piper.

"Hi, Daz. Got Syd, Steve and Becky on the line.

Put 'em through?"

Dazzle wished he had never learned how to work the speaker phone in Fred's cluttered office. He could feel his heart sinking when he replied, "Sure, I guess." Then counted to three, four.

"Daz honey!"

"Dazzy-sweetheart!"

"How's it hanging, hot stuff! You got our through-line yet? You ready to pitch this mother to the assholes upstairs?"

It was always more enthusiasm—and coming at him from more directions—than Dazzle could handle. Especially since Dazzle had never been what you might call an optimistic or forward-yearning sort of dog.

"It's, well, yeah," Dazzle said slowly, as if he were trying to lick a burr from his coat. "We're, you know. Really making progress and all that."

At which point, Dazzle permitted himself a hasty glance out the buggy window at Fred, who was sleeping off his third breakfast Margarita in the patio hammock.

"We're working out a few kinks, and developing the, what-do-you-call-it, the plot or something. And of course the central character—that is, *me*—he's getting more interesting by the minute. Hell, even *I'm* beginning to like him."

A long corporate hush emerged from telephone receiver like a voice from beyond the grave.

"Wow," it breathed.

"Cool."

"Bitchin'—I mean, that is, if you don't mind me using the word 'bitchin'? Is that okay with you, Dazzle-babe?"

There was so little you had to do to please these people, Dazzle thought.

"Absolutely fine," Dazzle said. "In fact, under these circumstances? Bitchin' is like the most perfect word there is."

"THE ONLY FREEDOM you ever really enjoy in this business," Fred liked to remind Dazzle, "is during the always-blissful period when nobody knows what you're doing. And the longer they don't know, the more freedom you've got. So here's how I interpret this contractual 'delivery calendar' you're so worked up about, Daz, and it goes like this. Sign the contract, get the bucks, and enjoy freedom freedom freedom, birdies singing, tra-la-la-la, la-la-la-*laaah*. Then deliver the pages, receive your delivery check, and it goes like this—hassle hassle hassle, mega-hassle mega-hassle, mini-hassles ad infinitum, talk talk talk, hassle hassle hassle. From the moment you give them what they say they want—which is the goddamn script they don't know what to do with—they'll be climbing up and down it like they've found themselves a new asshole. They'll turn it upside down and every which way. They'll schedule conference calls and studio meets, and before you know it, you'll have execs calling you from fucking Afghanistan and Tamaleland and places you never even knew existed, and they'll all be telling you what to do and how to do it. So stop worrying, my obedient little doggy. Chill out, enjoy the sea-breeze, and share some of these canned martinis. They're better than they look."

It was very annoying of Fred, Dazzle thought, to act as if he were some sort of "obedient" little doggy, when all he wanted to do was get the studio execs off his back. It was especially irksome that Fred did it with such eloquence and conviction.

"I'm not trying to sound like Mr. Obedient," Dazzle countered wearily. "I'm just trying to do the right thing. These jokers paid us a bundle, Fred. And we did agree to start delivering pages by, well, last month or something. I know they're jokers, and *you* know they're jokers, and believe me, I'm hip to the whole 'stop and smell the roses' philosophy. But you're not the guy who answers the phone around here. In case you forgot, these people are incredibly persistent. And to be fair, shouldn't we at least have a title by now? Or some minimal idea of the whaddayoucallit? The narrative arc?"

But of course Fred had already passed out in the hammock, a warm dented can of Make-U-Mix Chilled Martinis cradled against his chest like a begging cup.

It was so Fred, Dazzle thought. You couldn't help but like him.

DAZZLE LOVED THE beach. He loved the salty sand between his toe-pads, and the distant tease and crash of rubber-clad, seal-like surfers frolicking in the waves. He especially loved the air that felt both clean and astringent, as if the sea weren't simply providing an alternative to city soot, but was actually scrubbing away its residue, like swarms of hungry, eco-conscious animalculae. It was the perfect place for people without jobs, Dazzle thought.

"Like hey there, doggy-dude! How's the creativity-thing going? You should find a wet suit with four little doggy legs and I'll teach you to surf."

Diggy Bop was scrubbing his chapped, freckly face with waxy sun-screen and sucking diet soda from a can. At various times in their conversations, he had claimed to hale from the midwest, the east coast, the Gulf of Mexico, and the former Republic of Sudan, but most of the local surfers knew him as a native Whittier boy, born and bred. It was one of the few qualities Dazzle had learned to respect in these otherwise-unpalatable human biped types—the capacity to dissemble. The alternative seemed to be human beings who were perfectly happy with who they already were.

Yuck, Dazzle thought.

Dazzle sat down to rest beside Diggy Bop's stash of sandy boards and crumpled wet suits. "I'm afraid it's not going well at all," Dazzle conceded. "And to be perfectly frank, I don't think my so-called writing partner's giving it his best shot. All we seem to do is lie around the house watching TV."

Diggy Bop was looking at the vast Pacific. He had just finished his soda.

"Sometimes a guy's gotta wait for weeks to know what he's waiting *for*," Diggy said softly. "A girl, a wave, an inspiration. You can't go looking for it. It can only come looking for you."

At which point Diggy scooped up his board and sprinted towards a whitecap forming in the blue distance. Diggy wasn't much of a talker, Dazzle conceded. He was more of a doer.

And thank God for that, Dazzle thought.

BY THE TIME late afternoon came around, Dazzle had usually given up on receiving any help from Oscar-winning screenwriter and former Writer's Guild Assistant Secretary Fred Prescott, so he ventured alone into Fred's messy office and stared at the antique, dusty Selectra for a while. It was a peculiar, dense little machine with a revolving print-ball that Dazzle found infinitely amusing. What he didn't find amusing, however, was the alert thrum and snap the machine emitted whenever he activated the black power button, as if it had been waiting all morning for Dazzle to show up.

And now it was time for Dazzle to deliver the goods.

ACT I, Dazzle would type clumsily with his stubby, inarticulate fore-paw. SCENE 1. DAZZLE ENTERS. DAZZLE SPEAKS.

It was as far as Dazzle's imagination ever took him. Perhaps because the subject that least interested Dazzle was himself.

Dog meets bitch, Dazzle thought, recalling a notorious Faulknerian parable. Dog loses bitch. Dog finds bitch again.

Coming soon to a theater near you.

But sometimes, things don't tie up in a pretty little bow with appropriate theme music, Dazzle thought. Life just unravels until there's nothing left.

So then Dazzle deployed all of his worst narrative instincts. He thought about stupid movies he'd seen featuring big name stars grimacing in tight close-ups on multi-media-formatable movie posters. Like a grizzly, Bruce Willis sort of dog, with a flamethrower strapped to its back. Or a telegenic dog who plays basketball. He toyed with ideas of a precognitive dog, a flying dog, and a dog who saved children from imminent catastrophes. But try as he might, Dazzle couldn't get his creative juices flowing. And no matter how long he sat there trying to appease the hungry Selectric, he never once progressed beyond the same unhappy phrases:

DAZZLE ENTERS. DAZZLE SPEAKS.

Dazzle wished, Dazzle thought.

"Speak!" he told the Selectric. "Open your stupid maw and let it out!"

But, of course, machines don't talk. And dogs don't talk. Only human beings talk.

And that, in terms of Hollywood-style creative development, was the rub.

THE ONLY TIME Dazzle actually liked to hear the phone ring was when he sat down to do the work he couldn't do. Which was why he was always so quick to activate the desktop speaker–and utter the only word he could usually muster:

"Woof."

It didn't sound right even to Dazzle.

"Wow, Dad. You just fall out of the hammock or something? It's me, Benny. Your kid. Remember?"

It was the sort of voice Dazzle was accustomed to having directed his way. Short, curt sentences without modifiers. Simple animal expressions of calm and appeasement.

"Woof," Dazzle replied. "Woof woof."

"Gotcha, Dad. Know you're busy, just wanted to make sure you hadn't killed yourself with those damn TV dinners you're always stuffing down. Too bad I don't have any Hollywood connections. Maybe then I'd be worth your while for lunch or coffee or something. Or maybe even some minimally polite inter-personal conversation."

Click.

It was a lot of unlived life to live with, Dazzle thought, gazing out the window at somnolent Fred in his hammock, hearing the dial tone recommence like an endless, audible ellipses. Three divorces, four angrily neglected kids, seven undelivered scripts, a pending mega-deal at Paramount, and an irate Columbian lover with her own dry-cleaning service in Sepulveda. No wonder Fred got up so early each morning. It took a lot of time to get your head around doing so little.

You can't outlive bad karma like this guy's got, Dazzle thought.

You could only arrange to fall fast asleep before it came knocking.

UNLIKE PAGES, THE weeks were mounting up. And whenever Dazzle felt especially panicky about his contractual responsibilities, he called his agent.

"You got five minutes," Bunny said, her voice a deep echoing mine of patience with itself. "You speak and I'll listen. Shoot."

Bunny started off every conversation as if it were a race between Dazzle and her preconceptions about him. A race, of course, that Dazzle was always destined to lose.

"Oh, well," Dazzle muttered slowly. "Nothing new, really. I'm just getting nervous. We don't seem to be making any progress. And I don't mean to sound judgmental, but it's all Fred's fault. I was never born to write, Bunny. I'm just a goddamn dog. But Fred hasn't lifted a finger, and I think he may be burned out or something. So this is what I was thinking. Maybe we could just, you know, give them their money back, and I could go home to Big Sur. I'd even be willing to surrender all my rights to, you know, my life and identity. Really, I don't mind. Money's never mattered to me; basically, I'm happy with a few berries and wild mushrooms and a splash of clear spring water when I need it. I want my old life back, even if I don't own the rights to it anymore. So what do you say, Bunny? We tear up the contract, Sony brings in another, as they like to call it, 'creative team'. And we all go our separate ways."

Bunny's silence was potent enough to frost glass.

"Look, Daz-baby. We got you paid, right?"

"Well, yeah," Dazzle conceded. "But–"

"And now you're working with one of the most venerable and widely respected scriptwriters in the profession, right?"

"Sure, if you want to call Fred *venerable*, Bunny. It's just that–"

"So let me say one last thing, and listen to me good. I'd tear off my left tit before I gave Sony back a dime. I'd even tear off your balls, if you had any. So get back to work, and call me when you're ready to deliver. Otherwise, I'll turn you into the dog pound so fast it'll make your head spin. No offense, Darling. But I'm making you a Hollywood success story or my name ain't Bunny Fairchild."

IT WAS LIKE living with plutonium, Dazzle thought. The unwritten script emitted black radiance through every room in the house.

"I don't think you appreciate who you're working with," Diggy often told him, as they exchanged lukewarm cans of Coors over a sputtering, illegal campfire. "That's Fred Prescott on your team. He's like a filmic genius or something. He's like the only soulful person in the entire Hollywood community.

Why, a list of all the great movies he *could* have made would astound Michelangelo–at least that's how Fred tells it. Like his totally disrespected seven hundred page film treatment for *Finnegans Wake* starring Nick Nolte–*that* got totally dissed by the powers-that-be. Or what about Fred's genre-bending concept about a boxing-promoter on Mars? That got totally crummed on, too. Whenever the suits want to pretend they're artists, they hire Fred Prescott for a draft or two, and pat themselves on the back all over Rodeo Drive. Then they turn every script he delivers into a vehicle of mush for Hugh Grant and Drew Barrymore. But Fred endures the toil and struggle, Daz. He marches to the beat of his own drum. Give the guy a chance, and before this job's done? He's gonna teach you bozos what art is all about."

Dazzle wanted to believe Diggy–and in Diggy's vision of Fred. But the only way to believe in Fred was to disregard the daily pageant of shame and desuetude that constituted his 'routine.'

Art is never easy, Dazzle conceded. Maybe, just maybe, Fred knew what he was doing.

"Hey there, Daz baby. Stu Sanderson at Sony. Would you pick up the phone, Daz? We know you're in there. And we're totally sympathetic to your creative needs as an artist. But we really *gotta* touch base with you on one or two important concept points before we forget them. Isn't that what writing's about, Daz-baby? Writing down every little detail and pawing over it endlessly in high-power executive lunchrooms? Sally, have you got the concept points we discussed at yesterday's meeting? I need to read them to Daz here... Okay, point one–we need humor. Got that? It has to have *some* humor, Daz, but not *too much* humor, because comedy's not our department, but a *little* humor's okay, and actually pretty necessary, especially when it comes to talking dogs. Get me? Point two—and this is a little something Syd and I developed in our meeting with Roger last week—Daz is a dog, but he acts more like a cat. How do you like that one? Syd and I came up with that by ourselves. He's sort of a cat-like dog, with all these feline needs and desires and so forth, the audience will really eat it up. Like he digs catnip or something, or peeing in kitty litter—I'll leave the gory details to you creative types. We did this survey, or somebody heard about this survey, we're pretty sure a survey was done anyway, that says people are either cat people or dog people, and doing a dog movie alienates the cat-viewership and vice versa. So this way, we appeal to every possible demographic. We could sign any A-list director with a concept point like this one, Daz. You and Fred need to incorporate it into your treatment right away."

AS DAZZLE GREW less concerned about their long-broken contract deadlines, Fred slowly awakened from his stupor like a bewitched maiden in a castle. Some days, he even ventured out of his hammock before noon, and could be found browsing yesterday's sun-stained *Los Angeles Times* on the deck, or shoveling through a plate of Maria's huevos rancheros while tapping a pencil against a tablet of yellow fine-lined legal stationary. When he felt unusually perky, he cranked up his old LP-player and treated the beach-side sun-worshipers to a mega-decibel-blast of Stan Getz being mellow, or Paul Desmond pouring cool Hi-Fi martinis. It was like watching a space-captain emerge from suspended animation, Dazzle thought. He was still groggy and blood-sore. He couldn't quite work his lips.

"Hey, Fred," Dazzle would say as he padded to the kitchen, where Maria would stop brushing cobwebs off the ceiling with a damp mop, waddle to the stove, and happily scoop Dazzle's favorite lunch from a simmering pot: soft-shelled chicken tortillas with extra hot salsa and sour cream.

"*Mucho buenos, Señor Perocito,*" Maria liked to say, scratching between his ears, just the way Dazzle liked it. "*Escritor con Señor Fred es muy dificile, no?*"

Meanwhile, Fred examined the tip of his yellow Ticonderoga pencil with a piercing, level-headed gaze.

"The first thing you've got to do is walk away from what the world keeps telling you," Fred announced softly. "Like a penny saved is a penny earned, that sort of crap. Or how better mousetraps are always the rage, and the world will beat a path to your door. You don't need to be human to recognize human turds when you smell them, right, pooch? You just gotta clear your mind of all distractions and think for yourself

"WE'RE NOT TRYING to 'hound' you, Daz-honey. Get it? We're not trying to *hound* you?"

"We're just worried about the, you know, legal implications of all these delays and binding contractual clauses and modifying clauses which, you know, we can't just keep modifying. Unless there's an act of God or something."

"Nobody'd *hound* you, Daz baby. If it was an act of God–"

"But we need words, sweetheart. We need some–I

know you hate this word—but we need some *pages*. Syd isn't the most patient chief executive in town, but he's not the least patient, either. He's just doing his job, Daz. And whether you like it or not, we're just doing ours."

"We've got families to support."

"We've got wives, ex-wives, ex-semi-permanent live-in love-mates, and so forth. We're as human as the next guy. Which isn't to cast any aspersions on you, Daz baby. It's just an expression."

"Can we at least drive out and have a little meet at Cross Creek or something? We can watch Goldy play with her kids. You could show us some rough thoughts on a napkin and talk us through. You don't even have to tell Fred. It'll be our little secret."

"We could buy you a nice big bowl of naturally carbonated spring water. Or maybe a beer."

"And you could tell us, right, Daz-baby? You could finally tell us what this movie we're making is all about."

DAZZLE KNEW HIS days of Hollywood fame were numbered, so he tried to close the door securely on his way out. He instructed his accountant to dump his earnings into a series of 501ks and offshore investments. He set up a trust-fund for his ever-widening (and increasingly errant) canine family back in Big Sur, and arranged a lump sum guaranteed-annuity with a Hartford insurance firm. He gave himself a flea bath, had his nails clipped at the canine beauticians, and even endured what he hoped would be his last-ever full-body upper and lower GI polyp-palpating exam at the local vet, who turned out to be a well-groomed man in his mid-fifties named Dr.

Leroy Ferguson.

"I guess I moved here in the late sixties and never looked back," Dr. Ferguson confessed, as he gently posed and reposed Dazzle through a panoply of the usual indignities. "Where I came from, back in Ohio? We had nothing more interesting to do all day than go to the laundromat or visit the bank. Farmers would sit in Bob's Big Boy complaining about their cattle, or some leaky roof. And on your first (and often only) date, you drove to the woods in your third-hand car, screwed, got your girlfriend pregnant, and unhappily married, and not necessarily in that order. Personally, my only viable career choice was to become either a mortgage broker or a vet, and being a vet meant nothing but performing livestock viral exams and animal husbandry. You wouldn't see a decent doggy or kitty for weeks at a time. You were too busy driving across Farmer's Brown's scrub-strewn land in a truck. But then I got crazy and came to California, where everything was different. Suddenly, I was living with movie stars. I was spaying and neutering full-blooded manxes and siameses and even, I swear to god, an actual declawed leopard from Borneo once. And now my life is like a beautiful movie. I walk on the beach every morning, my kids go to great schools and marry entertainment lawyers and software executives, and my third wife, Patty, wow. She's got tits out to here and they're almost all hers. I have never felt more fulfilled as a veterinary surgeon and animal health-care-worker in my life, and my golf swing, Jesus. I'm knocking seagulls out of the air with my seven iron. I've gotten that good."

Even the doctor's hands, while they probed Dazzle's weary orifices, exuded confidence. It was like visiting one of those Shiatsu places at the mall. And when it was over, and Dazzle was gently lifted down from the paper-shielded metal table by a pair of bountiful young starlet-like nurses, he felt like a million bucks.

"I've just never met so many happy people in my life," Dazzle told Diggy over chocolatey cappuccinos at one of the Cross Creek picnic tables. "It's not like I originally pictured at all. I expected some sunny den of despair, where everybody's constantly enraged by the bastards who screwed them over on the last project that fell through. But when you look at Malibu for what it is, everybody has so much free time. Their nannies are taking care of the kids, their administrative assistants are answering the phones, and most of the time, all these people do is wander around clothing outlets, drive back and forth to Blockbuster, and eat lunch. In fact, now that I think of it, I hardly see any signs of depravity whatsoever, even from the sixty year old guys with twenty-something wives. They seem just as boring as everybody else. Except, of course, that they have a lot more money to be boring *with*."

BUT AS DAZZLE had learned from a lifetime of pissing on the lampposts of polite society, he always spoke way too soon. And the moment Diggy dropped him off at Fred's, he encountered a fleet of chickens coming home to roost simultaneously. These particular chickens were driving Arnold Schwarzenegger-style 'energy-efficient' re-tooled Humvees, decked-out PT Cruisers, and four-wheel drive off-road vehicles thumping with Wagner, Patti Smith, and mid-seventies progressive rock.

"We know you're in there, Pop!" shouted a twenty-something version of Fred in a linen sport coat and Levis. His features were so well-tended that they seemed shellacked. "You shut down, passive-aggressive, family-abandoning old hack! The worst part about hating guys like you, Dad, is that you never even show your face, or give us a chance to make fun of that hypocritical sixties get-up you wear! And then to hear you spouting all that outdated bullshit about marching to your own drum and beautifying the muse, Jesus! It makes me want to puke! You practically ruined my life, Dad! And if Mom hadn't met that property developer in Pasadena, you'd have ruined her life, too!"

The fleet of well-mobilized chickens represented the depth and breadth of middle-aged, middle-income California rage. Some of it, like Fred Junior's, had been fanned into a hot flame by years of assertiveness training and self-actualization therapy. But some of it had been twisted into bizarrely serene, flowery zen-like shapes by inner tranquility regimens and TM.

(To Dazzle's way of thinking, this second type of rage was the most frightening type of rage in the world.)

"We just stopped by to see how you're doing," Syd Fleishman said gently, flanked by various heads of development. "We're not like these other people. We're here to help. Maybe you'd be so kind as to let us in, Fred, and we could share some of our disillusioning experiences with the corporate entertainment industry. And then, you know, if you felt like it. Maybe you could show us some of the, ahem, you know. Some of the–"

"*Chingo tu madre*!" shouted the hot little Columbian

woman in a low-slung white cotton blouse and tight-fitting lime-green toreador pants. She was shaking a large loose pallet of ironed white shirts on a set of clattering wire coat hangers. "Take your dry cleaning and shove it straight up your butt, Fred Prescott! Screw you and your creative thought process–you miserable queer without balls!"

It was terrible, Dazzle thought, how bad karma could come revving into your driveway like this. It always seemed to know where you lived.

"You owe us for five months of gardening, Señor Piss-artist!"

"You stole my action concept at a Sizzler restaurant in Tustin, you lazy old ponce!"

"I bore you three children, listened to your endless pronouncements about art and liberty and beauty, and when it came to the settlement, you screwed me so bad I could hardly afford new sprinklers for the yard!"

"We only want to share the burden of creative development, Fred! We're not like all those other men in suits! We're here to help you make the most of your dreams and ambitions!"

Jesus Christ on a crutch, Dazzle thought. If life was a choice between these awful people and that filthy hammock, I'd probably be swinging my flea-bitten haunch in that hammock right now.

Then, as if a tiny displacement had occurred in the atmosphere, the entire crowd of belligerent shouters went totally quiet. And everybody blinked simultaneously at Fred's snail-tracked blue front door.

And watched the door open slightly–and a pale hand extrude, depositing a yellow foolscap legal pad on the thick brown horsehair doormat.

The door closed again. And like one thinking feeling organism, everybody looked directly at Dazzle.

IT TOOK DAZZLE a moment to catch up with all the attention. Then, once he caught his breath, he spoke the only word he had in him.

"Woof." Dazzle shrugged sheepishly. "Like what did you expect me to say?"

As if they were drawing a line with a laser, the crowd's attention moved slowly from Dazzle to the sheet of yellow foolscap paper on the doormat. And when they spoke, they spoke through one individual at a time.

"Who's the dog?"

"*El perro es muy* exacerbating."

"I told you I smelled something special about that mutt. I don't know what it is exactly, but I'm pretty sure I like it."

"I didn't even know Dad had a dog. All my life, as a kid, I'm begging for a dog. But he never gets one until I'm already grown up."

Feeling self-conscious, Dazzle trotted across the brown lawn, picked up the legal pad with his teeth (he hated when dogs did stuff like this), trotted over with apparent dutifulness to Syd Fleishman of Sony Pictures Tristar, Inc, and lay it down at his feet.

"I think," Dazzle said humbly, "that this is what you came for."

The suits separated from the crowd like the yolk from an egg.

"What's it say?"

"It's definitely Fred's handwriting. But it's hard to read."

"That's a tee and that's an aitch and that there—"

"Through-line. It says through-line. And right after that. It's a date."

Then Syd came forward–pushing everyone out of his way.

"I pay you guys to think and you can't even read." He held up the yellow legal pad like Moses carrying tablets down from the mountain. And then he told everybody what it said.

> *Cool dog. Cool guy. Buddy pic. Big shots get thrown out of buildings, set on fire, the works. Politically conscious, eco-wary, funny with a heart. Explosive finale, two week pre-opening ad campaign on VH-1, Family Network and Animal Planet. 60 mill opening–***secure***.*

It was as if the entire crowd of gang-haters gasped at once. Everybody waited for somebody to say something. Finally, somebody did.

"You're the fucking *man*," Syd whispered under his breath, holding the sheet of yellow foolscap in the air like an Olympic torch.

And slowly, like a chant, the entire crowd began whispering it too.

"IT'S LIKE I always said," Dazzle explained to Diggy, on the day he was dropped off at the Burbank Greyhound station. "I'm not cut out for the writerly life. I don't have creative genes or something. The worrisome part is that I don't even recognize a decent writer when I meet one. Seriously, I had Fred pegged as a tiresome old hack with delusions of grandeur, but what do I know? Now, without any help from me (his supposed inspiration) he's taken our script to 'the next level', as Stu put it. They're bringing in six-figure rewrite teams. They're coordinating tri-agency talent deals to develop, cross-market and cast. And the concept's so hot it's being passed around at pool parties and Bar Mitzvahs, and all I ever did was answer the phone, lie to people I don't know, and walk on the beach."

Diggy's car was littered with fast food wrappers, expired bottles of sun screen, and yellowing dead-winged pages of the *Los Angeles Times* and *Coast Mall Shopper.* You could perform a fairly accurate sociological survey in this screwy Toyota, Dazzle thought. The ratio of fast-food franchises to miles driven by the average surfer, or something totally useless like that.

"I told you, Daz. Fred doesn't compromise, dig? He remains totally faithful to his beautiful muse."

It was the smoggiest day Dazzle could remember, and the funny thing was? It had never looked more beautiful or benign. Pink and orange and purplish clouds rimmed the horizon, like one of those multi-layer liquer-cocktails served as lady-drinks in phony, overpriced west-side bars.

"Yeah, well, maybe you're right, Diggy," Dazzle concluded wistfully. "And I'll definitely never remember good old Fred without smiling. What a life. What a profession. I guess somebody's got to do it. I'm just glad it's not me."

"Looks like your bus, Dude. You come visit soon and I'll teach you to boogie board. It'll be awesome."

It was the best part about any animal, Dazzle thought. The part that got enthusiastic about things. (Even boogie boards.)

"I'll do that, Diggy," Dazzle said sincerely, as he climbed out of the car. "And if you ever make it to

Big Sur? I'll teach you the only thing I know anything about. And that, of course, would be taking really long and meaningful naps."

"Do what you do best, dude. Or don't do nothing at all."

And of course Diggy, as always, was right.

7. DAZZLE SPEAKS WITH THE DEAD

DAZZLE WAS NEITHER a mystical nor a metaphysical sort of dog. He didn't believe in karma, redemption, the transcendental ego, or the immanence of Platonic forms. For Dazzle, the world was a meaningless and immutable mess–and the byproduct of entirely material insufficiencies. Not enough bones to go around, say. Or people with too many weapons living next door to people without any. So it came as something of a surprise when Dazzle developed, late in life, a gift for speaking with the dead. He had never sought out such a gift, but once it came his way, he lived with it the best that he could.

"I want to tell her that I'm sorry I didn't clean the bowl more often, or show her enough attention, especially when I was working," Mr. Lapidus confessed to Dazzle in the sandalwood-scented Comfort-Room of Madame Velma's Spiritual Contact

Center, the longest-functioning spiritual arts shop on the central coast. "I meant to clean it more often, but I never did. And I wish I'd been more affectionate. I don't know how affectionate I could've *been* with a goldfish, but I should've at least made more of an effort. I'm just not the sort of person who develops healthy emotional connections with other creatures, probably because I didn't know my father when I was little. Other little boys had fathers to play with but I never did."

Dazzle was accustomed to the weeping, the frantic hand-wringing, and the physical convulsions that manifested human remorse. But if he lived to be a thousand, he would never grow accustomed to the preposterous get-up that Madame Velma insisted he wear each morning while "serving" customers: the multicolored scarves layering his forehead like the turban of some furry Sikh, or the silver-painted bracelets chiming loosely from his neck and ankles, making him feel like a cheap whore at a carnival.

Sitting on a rickety wooden stool behind an even ricketier card table, Dazzle took a deep breath, closed his eyes, and placed his callused paws against the sides of his gloaming, Taiwanese-manufactured crystal ball.

"*Shhhh,*" Dazzle breathed softly. "Somebody's trying to speak."

Mr. Lapidus, wringing his large pale sweaty hands, hunched closer.

"Yes, I'm listening," Dazzle whispered. "Speak louder, please. Your name's Fishface and you're lonely. Your name's Fishface and you're trying to find a path into the next world."

Mr. Lapidus blew his nose into a moppy clump of Kleenex, his eyes round and wide.

"Have you found my beloved Fishface?" he asked. "How did you know her name? What's she trying to say?"

Dazzle cautioned Mr. Lapidus with his half-lidded eyes.

"Life *was* hard," Dazzle confirmed. The spectral presence appeared in Dazzle's ambient perception like a blip on a sonar screen, a spiny blur of incoherency and loss. "It was cold and round and came up hard from every direction. It yielded nothing but the minimal reflections of yourself."

Mr. Lapidus stopped crying and sat up straight. He could feel the presence too. Or maybe he could just feel Dazzle feeling it.

"And now all you're looking for is peace," Dazzle continued, trying not to look directly at Mr. Lapidus. "You aren't interested in what this lonely man wants from you. You just want to get as far away from his big, emotionally-obsessed moon-face as you can get."

SINCE APPOINTING DAZZLE her Apprentice-Medium-in-Training, Madame Velma had departed to Club Med with a Dominican leaf-blower named Hymie Sanchez. But not before signing over the DBAs to her financial manager, and opening an online account at the downtown Albertsons, where Dazzle could purchase home-delivered dog food, fresh fruit and vegetables, and an occasional mixed-case of Côte du Rhône or Beaujolais nouveau–which proved especially useful in helping Dazzle unwind after a long day communing with the cosmos.

"They don't really care one whit about their recently-departed," Madame Velma assured him during their weekly phone conference, her voice suffused with the immanent echoey rush of waves on what Dazzle envisioned as a white, shell-less beach framed by blue sky and bluer water. "They just can't stand being disobeyed. People develop an unnatural attachment to pets, mainly on account of pets got no say in the matter. Go there, sit here, eat this, sleep on the floor, get in the cage, stop growling–people always get what they want from the human-beast dynamic, and that's extremely satisfying to the sorts of fragile egos that need pets. But when a pet dies, it issues the only independent statement it ever makes, as in: 'Good riddance, pal! Take your catnip toys and doggy treats and shove 'em straight up your you-know-what!' It's like primal disobedience at the cellular level. For pet-lovers, it sends their self-images into a state of shock. They can't believe it's happening. Suddenly, their pets have become as indifferent to their happiness as everybody else."

Since developing an evening regimen of lapping moderately-priced wine from a plastic dog bowl, Dazzle had grown about as mellow as he was likely to get.

"I'm cool on the whole over-the-top emotional crisis deal," he said, kicking back on Madame Velma's corrugated blue sofa amongst the burbling lava lamps and steadily glimmering Hummels. "I'm even cool with the neediness, the endless litany of personal regret, and the desperate post-midnight pleading for emotional guidance when, jeez, you know me, Velma. I don't care what happens to human beings–I really don't. But the part that drives me most crazy is that here I sit, day after day, listening to one homo-sap after another begging me to contact their departed loved ones and then, when I *do* make contact? They're not interested in what their loved ones are trying to say. They just carry on whining about what *they're* feeling, and *their* pain, as if the entire spiritual universe is all about *them.*"

Unlike Dazzle, who tended to worry too hard about things, Madame Velma was more the carpe-diem type personality. Which was probably why her voice faded away into the distant rush of waves whenever Dazzle's voice grew most distraught.

"*Te amo, mamacita,*" a swarthy-sounding Latin voice whispered in the staticky background, as rhythmic and self-sustaining as the tides of St. Tropez. "*Te amo* all the time."

But if Dazzle waited long enough, Velma either hung up the phone, or reemerged from what sounded like a long kiss.

"You've got a gift, Daz," Madame Velma would conclude, "whether you like it or not. Me, I was a total charlatan, with all those spooky hidden tape machines and wobbly floorboards hooked to remote controls and so forth. But I know a good soul when I meet one and one of those good souls happens to be yours. So do what your gift tells you, honey, and always remember the most important part of spiritual-arts services: we take cash, money orders, and American Express, but never Visa. Those Visa pricks keep hitting us with surcharges, and if there's one thing that pisses off Madame Velma, it's lining pockets that aren't hers."

SOMETIMES THE WAITING room at Madame Velma's grew so crowded with tearful comfort-seekers clutching hand-worn animal toys and framed photographs that Dazzle resorted to a crude fire-hydrant-red Take-a-Number dispenser at the front door.

"Okay, Number Seven-Six-Six, let's cut to the chase. Your cat got crushed by a semi, and he's been searching purgatory for months but can't find his catnip bell anywhere. My advice, as per usual, is burn it. Help Sheba understand there's nothing worth coming back for, and she'll stop waking you in the night with her infernal mewling, and knocking over the rubbish bins. Oh, and by the way, she does sometimes miss you a tiny bit. She recalls you as the Bringer of Meat, and the Warmth That Lingers in Cushions, which is pretty good individuation for a cat. Those characters usually never think about anybody but themselves. *Next!*"

"Rightie-oh, so we're up to Seven-Six-Seven, and I can't help you if you don't listen, so listen good. Polly didn't want a cracker—she just wanted you to stop clipping her wings long enough so she could fly out that window as far as she could get. She didn't like your smell, she didn't like your taste in music, and she definitely didn't like your girlfriend, who, by the way, bludgeoned poor Polly to death with a meat tenderizer and carefully positioned the corpse in front of that carefully blood-smeared window so you'd think what she wanted you to think. My advice is to dump the broad, let Polly carry on her quest for non-being, and get on with your life while you still got one. *Next!*"

"Which brings us to Number Seven-Six-Eight—jeez, what time is it, anyway? You've got exactly two minutes and here goes. You had a hamster and it died, big fucking wow. That's what hamsters do, pal, so get used to it. Believe me, Kiddo appreciated the little world you built for her with mazes and skytowers and tubal corridors and so forth. But now she's roaming the stratosphere with all the other dead hamsters, and it's time to let go. So please, fill that plastic bottle for me with this budget-priced Cuernavaca, and hook the pipette to my collar–there's a little clasp right there next to my license. Oh, and slip the Nachos into my shoulder flap, that's the ticket. I'm off to the beach where I'm planning to get really, really drunk. And please turn off all the lights when you leave. If Madame Velma ever catches sight of our latest utility bill, she'll kick my sorry ass into the Great Beyond her damn self."

WHAT DAZZLE MOST appreciated about the beach was the way it scrubbed the air clean of implications–concepts like identity, meaning, specificity and permanence didn't mean much out here, where everything that ever *was* was continually being eroded into everything it *wasn't* and back again: driftwood and condoms, broken sea shells and pop-bottles, seagull poop and cigarette butts, jetsam and flotsam, forth and so forth. The sensory freedom was exhilarating, Dazzle thought, gazing up at the heavy moon and fractal stars. Every smell and sound and texture seemed to be wrapped up in everything else, like some Dionysian schiz-bath of pure undifferentiated sensation.

"It's the only place where I can hear myself think anymore," Dazzle confessed to his friend Harry Canfield, a publicly-disgraced family-investment adviser who had recently begun sleeping under the pier in a moldy goose-down mummy-bag, "and escape all that endless wittering of dead pets yearning for the crappy plastic doodads they left behind. Like rubber chew toys. Or hamster wheels. Or, jeez, their filthy litter boxes–if that isn't a metaphor for enslavement by material crap, I don't know what is. It makes me wonder, Harry. What's it gonna be for me when I'm dead and almost gone–diminishing in the stellar radiance like some dissipating radio signal from *What's My Line?* What will I be endlessly desiring back on this increasingly perilous and desperate ball of dirt and stupidity and grief? My comfy sofa cushions? My sweet spot in the Big Sur cave next to Edwina? Or will it be my emerging fondness for alcohol, which is the only thing that makes me relax anymore? Is *that* all I've got to look forward to when I cash in my chips? Nothing like redemption or consolation or surcease from sorrows. Just the emerging bitter need for something that never really needed me back. My dog license. My IRAs and ISAs. Things and more things, stuff and more stuff. Because if that's what living is all about, Harry, then maybe we should just call an end to the whole shabby shebang right now."

Harry was crouched fondly over a thinly blazing can of Sterno with a pair of hotdogs skewered on a twisted coat hanger. It was one of Harry's endearing qualities, Dazzle had come to realize: his ability to appreciate life's simplest pleasures.

"As I get older, you know what I think about, more and more? That old Toyota Corolla my parents gave me when I graduated college," Harry reflected softly. "Palomino white with white sidewall tires; it never broke down once in five years. And an eight-track tape deck back before eight-track tape decks were funny. Sometimes, I miss that damn car more than my kids, my house, my wife, or even–and I hope you pardon the expression—or even my stupid dog. It was certainly more dependable than the rest of them put together."

As on most Avila Beach nights, stars sprayed the sky like a phosphorescent aerosol mist. They were almost too real, Dazzle thought. All those infinite pinpricks of light that embodied unencompassable vastnesses.

"It's funny the things we hold onto," Dazzle said. The hot dogs were turning black and bubbly in places—just the way he liked them. "And I don't mean ha-ha funny. I mean just funny in a *philosophical* sense."

Harry had hit the last economic downturn like a drunken speedboat against Morro Rock. One moment, he was bathing in the splendor of dewy-eyed Hollywood starlets and their thirty-something, UCLA-graduated managing agents, channeling their six-figure advances into investment-portfolios and never-say-die ponzie schemes, coking himself to the gills on the purest Bolivian Cloud-rock, and dancing on the hoods of stretch limos from Zuma to Marin— the next moment he was being locked out of his beachfront mansion by his wife, his wife's still-teen surfer-boyfriend (a six-figure-per-session underpants model named Rory Klein) and his beloved twin daughters, Staci and Chanel. For Harry, life was a lot like death: an endless series of remembrances about how good things *use* to be.

"That fucking Toyota started up like a dream and never failed me once," Harry said out loud, stoking his driftwood campfire with a piece of charred, twisted wood. "Unlike my wife, or my kids, or that whole derivative scheme that sucked me up along with half the whiz-kids at J.P. Morgan. I don't know about you, dog, but while I don't miss much about my sad material existence, that Toyota definitely tops the list."

DAZZLE USUALLY WOKE to the pre-dawn clamor of beeping garbage trucks along the boardwalk, and the exhortations of Mad Alice walking her shaggy, muttish dogs along the thinning bright shoreline in her baggy gray Mexican wool sweater and leather sandals.

"Six ayem, boys!" Mad Alice shouted, striking each of them three metronomic beats on the butt with her varnished redwood walking stick. "The shore patrol hits these sands at six thirty, and you need to kick sand over this campfire, and move your legs long enough so you don't qualify as loiterers! Now, if you're hungry, there's day old donuts and coffee out back of the Beachfront Café. And if you hurry, I spotted some cinnamon muffins amongst the usual French style. You're still a cinnamon muffin sort of dog, aren't you, Daz?"

With dawn came more than recollection, Dazzle thought. As the pinkish morning glow diminished into the flat blue horizon, the voices of departed entities regained focus and resolution in little bursts of static, like Russian or Chinese radio broadcasts hitting the dashboard radio in the post-midnight resonance. "I want my squeaky ball under the sofa in the den," whispered an expired Pomeranian named Dodo, somewhere off Grover Beach. Or: "Those breadcrumbs look delicious"–emanating from a forlorn spectral pigeon fluttering eternally over the 101 overpass in Goleta. Departed spirits popped and

sparked in the air around Dazzle's brain like tiny
fireworks or tiny blizzards of sentience. "Give me
bring me get me need need need. I want want want
must must must must. Help me help me find me help
me."

"After I lost Frankie Avalon the Third," Alice
confessed later, sharing charity donuts and coffee on
the greatest beachfront bench in the history of
civilization (or so Dazzle figured), "I thought my life
was over. I went to bed thinking about that stupid
dog and woke up thinking about him. For months, I'd
jump out of bed and head straight to the kitchen and
start fixing his breakfast before I stopped and
thought, 'Hey. What the hell am I doing? Frankie's
dead as a doornail. He got a tumor on his liver and
the chemotherapy never took.' He was dead for
months and wouldn't go away, and something in me
wouldn't let him go away, it was like we were bound
together in some diminishing spiral of being and
nothingness all at once. The carpets were still brown
with his damn dog hairs. There were still these round
ovular stains where he'd throw up on the corduroy
sofa after eating crap off the beach. And then the
voice of that dog would start buzzing around in my
head. 'Go for walkies!' he kept saying. 'Give me treat
and go for walkies!' It was like I could hear his voice
bouncing around the house in the places he used be.
Near the front door, in the kitchen near his doggy
bowl, out back near the gate. 'Go for walkies! Beach
beach beach! Run on sand. Eat crap off beach!' It
was like that crazy dog had a one-track mind and that
one-track mind was circulating endlessly through my
house like those automatic floor sweepers, you know
the kind I mean? They look like little silver robo-dogs

but they do the vacuuming. The kind that were invented by the Japanese."

AFTER BREAKFAST, ALICE drove Dazzle back to SLO in her '86 Ford Ranger S. Otherwise he might miss his first appointments at Madame Velma's, which started heating up around nine or nine-thirty.

"You can't spend your life living for the dead, hon," she told Dazzle one morning. Her face was as wrinkled as the underlay of a cardboard box, and she squinted against the yellow sun as if she were being struck by a continual revelation. "You may not have noticed, but you aren't looking so good since you started drinking and working weekends. Maybe it's time to hang up your crystal ball and get your butt back to planet Earth."

At Madame Velma's, they were already in the waiting room, holding up their yellow number-tags like over-eager suitors at a flash-date.

There was Mr. Lapidus, of course, with his mineral-streaked goldfish bowl, and Mrs. Judson, with her rhinestone-studded dog collar. Or the Burley Brothers, carrying the rusty cage of their departed ferret, Sparky, between them like pallbearers at a children's zoo; or Miss Muñoz, weeping into the faded flannel scarf of her dead burro, Maximilian Buonaparte the IV. Gathered together in Madame Velma's tastelessly over-decorated ante-room, they resembled the most random conglomeration of humanity any fool dog could possibly imagine: lonely, bereft, and lugging around all the crap that once divided them from their animal familiars. Some days, entering Madame Velma's anteroom felt like entering a flea-market in hell. Everybody had something to sell but nobody in their right mind wanted to buy it.

"Mr. Dazzle? Are you in contact with Fishface? You've got that faraway look in your eyes–like you're looking at me and you're not looking at me. It's the sort of look I've been getting all my life. It's me, Mr. Lapidus. Look, I'm first in line, and I been waiting since four a.m. I just remembered something important to tell Fishface. It's about the noise from my television, which even the neighbors complain about. All those gunshots and torture sounds from *CSI* and so forth. I can't stop thinking about how terrified she must have been with all that endless high-volume violence echoing around her fishbowl. It kept me up all last night. So much to be scared about and so little time to understand–isn't that what life's really about, Mr. Dazzle? And then, just when we start to understand a tiny bit of it? We're suddenly dragged off to some other meaningless form of non-existence altogether."

THEN, ONE NIGHT when he least expected it, Dazzle was visited by a spirit from his own half-forgotten life–and not, as usual, a spirit from the half-forgotten life of others.

"Dazzle, honey? Can you hear me? It's Mom. It's very dark out here, and I'm having trouble finding you and your sisters. I can smell you, but I can't see you. Is that our garbage bin over there? It's even darker and scarier-looking than usual. Can you help me find my way? This is a lot more complicated than it should be. After all, I'm just looking for our silly old garbage bin. I'm just looking for my babies."

Now Dazzle was not a sentimental sort of creature; in fact, he considered "sentiment" to be one of those bourgeois illusions that bound animals up in fantasies of individual plenitude and fulfillment. But when he heard that unmistakable voice–and smelled that unmistakable smell–a surge of emotion rose from his chest as swift and disorienting as one of the legendary riptides off the Pacific Coast. When first it takes your ankle, it feels flirtatious. But then, before you know it, it wraps you up in stronger arms than yours, and drags you into dimensions you can't control.

"Mom?" Dazzle said. It was one of those words he never expected to use again and somehow, in the simple act of using of it, he felt something round and pliable burst inside him, and wetness spilling out of his face and heart like an overflowing of the world he had always secretly and profoundly loved. "Mom?" The tears were like a physical convulsion; they shook Dazzle to his core–and then shook him again.

Like many precocious children, Dazzle suffered from conflicted memories of his mother, who had raised him the best she could behind a Ralph's Market in Encino, and then went off on a wander, got hit by a bus, and unknowingly relegated him to the dubious patronage of the Los Angeles SPCA. In his earliest, most intensely-remembered days and nights of existence, she had been pure surfeit and totality, dispensing milk and love and indulgence and marveling at every aspect and expression of him. "You're so handsome," she told him. "You're so smart. You're so much better than your father. You're my baby, you're my lover, you're my honey, you're my all all all. I'll hold you close forever, baby. Your mommy loves you more than anything."

And then you went away, Dazzle thought, the

tears pouring out of him like water from a faucet. You loved me and promised me and then you went away.

It was so selfish to hate her for her mortality, he thought. But it was the only thing he *could* hate her for. And it was the only way he could get her back.

It took him several minutes to catch his breath. He sat up on the living room couch. He gazed into the empty air.

"I don't know how to tell you this, Mom. But you're dead. You don't exist. You're like this reflection that keeps reflecting after the mirror is broken, or this echo of a voice that has gone away but keeps echoing. You don't have any more substance than that, Mom. And you'll never have any more substance than that ever again."

There were other voices out there, Dazzle realized. Ducks, walruses, ostriches, ocelots, kangaroos, pandas—even human beings. A discordant continually accumulating cacophony of intentions and desires and memories and misfortunes. It was like stumbling into a huge subterranean vault filled with the newspapers of a dead civilization, bristling with an infinity of DOW forecasts, midnight TV schedules, astrological horoscopes, crossword puzzles and op-ed features about elections, weather-paradigms, international treaties and scientific discoveries that no longer mattered because everybody who once pretended to care about them were dead. And in the midst of all that black-and-white hieroglyphic unreadability, a small spark of color flashed. It called out to Dazzle's peculiar and unwanted extra-sensitivity. It had a name.

"You have seven sisters," Mom said, "but I love you best. You're my big boy. We keep each other

147

warm behind the garbage bin, Dazzle. Please don't send me away."

It didn't seem fair, Dazzle thought. All this unwanted emotion spilling out of him, tracking his gray chest hair with tiny sand-speckled rivulets. How could he send her away?

Because he couldn't send her away until he knew how much he wanted her back.

He wanted her back.

And then he could send her away.

"IT'S NEVER EASY to tell who's holding onto whom, or why we can't let go," Dazzle explained a few nights later to his assembled soon-to-be-former clients at a pre-announced "Going Out of Business Spiritualist Confab" on the post-midnight Avila shore. "Even when we know better, we try to hold onto what we can't keep. That's because the most horrible realization any self-reflective creature can suffer is that this whole crazy universe doesn't make sense, even on a good day. It doesn't make sense that what we love can't last; and that, in the long run, we can't ourselves last for those we love. What sort of fucking asshole universe is that? It's a fucking asshole universe, that's what it is. And I'm sick of it."

Gathered together on the darkling beach, Dazzle's clients represented every conceivable shape, size and ethnicity, brightly adorned in dashikis and fezzes and Native American headdresses and mandala-earrings and peacock-emblazoned Indian saris. And, like most New Agers of the late baby-boom generation, they seemed mutually ill-fitted to their exterior manifestations. It's like they're dressing to be somebody they've never met, Dazzle often thought.

Someone infinitely wise with all the answers. Someone who will live forever.

"What does that even *mean*?" Mr. Lapidus whined miserably, clutching his mildewy ceramic castle as if it were the only safety bar on a vertiginously careening roller coaster. "What do you mean the universe doesn't make sense–what sort of comfort is *that*? And of course we can hold onto the ones we love–you help us do it every day. Why are you trying to confuse us just when we're starting to find a little peace in this terrible world where everybody's always dying, even me?"

Mr. Lapidus's big, red, tear-streaked face was like a worm on a picnic table. Everybody had to look at it, and as soon as they looked at it, they looked away. Mrs. Beasley with her squeaky rubber dinosaur. Mrs. Cha with a blue corrugated Kong. Freddy Watson with a mouse-shaped catnip toy. Louisa Merchant with a heavily scored cuttlebone. Too often, Dazzle thought, our lives record the passage from one piece of meaningless crap to another. And there's no end to the things we can't throw away.

"What I'm trying to tell you, Mr. Lapidus–and all you fine, bereaved people–is that I've been going about this whole sixth-sense nonsense the wrong way. I tried to give everybody what they asked for–contact with the lost friends who left them. I tried to help you adjust to their departures with this one-step-at-a-time approach. But, as I'm finally learning, the one-step-at-a-time approach never works. If you want to actually change your life, it's gotta be cold turkey."

AS A PUP, Dazzle had been briefly enamored of Sixties rock music, especially the Woodstock-types such as Carlos Santana and Stephen Stills. It had all seemed so simple back then: just take off your clothes, roll around in the dewy grass, smoke a little doobage, and love whoever you were with. For decades, public media had dismissed those brief muddy years as a sort of bizarre, Manson-like orgy of crime, freaky sunglasses, and a pathological disregard for the achievements of supply-side economics. But Dazzle remembered them fondly as a fragrant period of benign inattention. Love the one you're with, Dazzle thought now. Ignore all the bullshit and politicians and stupidity and guns and bombs. If you can't be with the one you love, baby—just love the one you're *with*.

"We've all got our crosses to bear," Dazzle told his spiritually-distraught customers. "We've all got things we want back, and voices we don't want to lose, and a faith in ourselves that we'll never have again. Which is why I want to do this together. It's time for everybody to let go, especially me. It's time to take what was never ours and set it free. So I want you all to grab hold of whatever it is you want back, and feel what it feels like one more time. That paltry little object, or that memory, or that still-resonant voice in your head. Then I want you to turn to whoever's standing next to you and do the only thing left to do for any sane, rational individual in a totally insane, irrational universe."

Dazzle paused for healthy dramatic effect.

"Swap," he said.

It was so obvious, he thought. I don't know why I didn't think of it before.

"SO WHAT HAPPENED *then?*" Mad Alice asked,

turning over three pasty-colored tofu-patties on a tinily blazing Walgreens brand Hibachi with a long metal fork. She had recently done something dreadlocky to her whitish-gray hair that made her look like an inverted mop.

Lying on his favorite green khaki blanket, Dazzle gazed at the glowing coals with a pleasant sense of inanition. *When things get hot enough, all things turn into something else,* he thought. *Even something as unpalatable-looking as a tofu-patty.*

"What else *could* they do?" Dazzle shrugged. "It's hard to ignore somebody who speaks with this voice of authority I've developed. It's a voice I plan to jettison the first chance I get."

Harry poured three paper cups full of fruit smoothies from a large glass pitcher–a concoction of icily whipped bananas, mangoes, granola, kiwi and lemon zest that Mad Alice had dubbed the Banana Wow! Ever since releasing his clients three days ago, Dazzle had submitted to Alice's most stringent self-purging program–nothing but fresh fruit, vegetables, and, every night before bed, a large glass of pure unfiltered lemon juice.

"So," Dazzle continued, "Mrs. Chen dutifully swapped her costume-jewelry encrusted kitty collar for Mr. Jorgensen's hamster-car. And Phil Hatland swapped his budgie bell for Harriet's well-chewed sweat-sock. And rubber balls got swapped with squeaky toys and doggy treats got swapped with fish-flakes and one sense of loss got swapped with another sense of loss and one memory got swapped with another memory and, before you knew it, everybody was talking and chattering about these terribly insignificant items and dead beasts and crying and hugging and feeling some reasonable measure of catharsis in the arms of one another. It was like this really embarrassing group hug and, to be totally frank, I indulged in some of the 'good vibes' myself. I mean, there we were, sharing in this really awkward sense of togetherness and well-being, and suddenly I look up from this great scratch I'm receiving between the ears from a hand I can't recognize to find the one lonely soldier on the shore, looking like a wallflower at the orgy. Poor, rubbery-red-faced Mr. Lapidus, clutching that stupid ceramic castle and looking like he's about to burst. And nobody wants to go near him, right, since he's a walking exemplification of everything we've left behind–that sense of solitary loss we feel cringing alone in the dark. And I don't know what happened, but I just stared Mr. Solitary Loss straight in the eye, walked up to him, and took that silly ceramic castle from his white-clenched fingers with my teeth. He wanted to let go; he wanted to give it to me; but his fingers took some convincing. And when I finally flung that stupid ceramic castle into the campfire where it belonged, neither of us turned to watch it burn. Instead, I stood as tall as I could on these old gray hind legs and gave Mr. Lapidus the last thing Mom gave me before we parted material company forever. And Mr. Lapidus thanked me in just the way I expected.

"'*Ewwwww*,' he said, wiping his mouth as if he had just tasted mandrill-poop. 'I got licked on the mouth by a *dog!*'

"Frankly, it was a lot less thanks than I deserved. And at the same time, considering the fundamental ingenerosity of human beings? It was all the thanks I could ever expect.

8. STARSHIP DAZZLE

AT AN AGE when most dogs are contemplating retirement by a shaggy fireside, or the looming possibility of euthanasia in the rubber-gloved embrace of some smirking vet, Dazzle convinced the National Aeronautics and Space Administration to send him into space on a rocket. He wasn't sure how he did it, either. He just presented his case before a tableau of diet soda-swilling, weirdly-bearded scientists, and once he was finished, they couldn't seem to launch him into the stratosphere soon enough.

"I know I haven't been the best company you could wish for on this stupid planet," Dazzle explained to the audience of low-rung journos, technical support staff, and corporate-sponsor spokespersons on the day of his departure. His makeshift canine space-suit, sewn together from a motley arrangement of past-shelf-life remnants, resembled a jumble-sale of bubble-wrap, twisted wire coat hangers and aluminum siding. "And I'm sure you'll be perfectly happy to see my hairy butt vanish into the Pleiades. But at the same time, I'm not bitter about our past dealings, and I hope you're not bitter about me either. So good luck, try to clean up the mess you've made of this planet, and think about me every so often. By the way, my name is Dazzle, and while you probably can't tell from this crazy space suit I'm wearing, I'm a dog. I'm taking off in that rocket-ship over there, and if I run into any alien space mercenaries while I'm out there, I'll tell them, Hey! Don't even think about attacking those yokels back where I come from, or enslaving them in some cosmic chain-gang–however much they deserve it. Fact of the matter is they're armed to the gills with over-priced weaponry and don't mind using it. On you or each other–it's all the same to them."

IT WASN'T A dignified departure. They simply hooked him up to a squeaky winch and swung him into the nose of the roughly-hewn command module, as perfunctorily as if they were loading a crate of wire-bound newspapers into the back of a van.

They didn't even offer a proper goodbye.

"**...ten, nine, eight...**" said a tinny, staticky voice in Dazzle's head-set.

"Hey, wait!" Dazzle, who had never before suffered any form of government-subsidized public transportation, couldn't help feeling a healthy dose of control-or-be-controlled anxiety. "Did you lock that hatch? We got potable water on this tug? Where's the Cheetos? When I signed onto this gig, they promised me something called Liquefied Cheetos, but I just realized something! I don't know what the hell that is!"

"**...four, three, two...**"

"And another thing–is this doodah being

televised? Or do they even cover space-launches anymore? If you're listening–Dad, Edwina, kids–I love you all. I know it isn't very responsible of me to go traipsing off across the universe, but it's something I *gotta* do!"

Dazzle's farewell was drowned out by a thunderous explosion. Strapped into the poorly-padded bucket-seat, he rattled amongst the steel-framed dashboard components like a set of false teeth in a broken doll.

"**Ignition!**"

Until there was only one thing left for Dazzle to say:

"Jesus H. Christ!"

He couldn't even hear himself saying it.

He could only count on the very likely fact that he did.

DAZZLE DREAMED HE was being compressed into a gigantic tin can by a machine with jagged chrome gears and spring-loaded levers. "I'm not a goddamn piece of tuna!" he kept shouting, with dream-like regularity. "I'm a dog with his own unique character and personality!"

But the machine, like all machines, didn't care about dogs. It just crunched and ratcheted and spumed. After a while, Dazzle awoke in the trembly cockpit, shaking like a cat at the vet.

"Hey!" Dazzle whispered, cotton-mouthed, into the intimacy of his headset. "What's a guy got to do to get a drink of water in this place?"

Various digital displays blinked cyberishly from the wide, complicated dashboard. And through the curved perspex windows, stars emerged like fireflies.

And that–out there–luminous and bloated and enormous, what the hell was that? An alien spacecraft, a meteor, a cloud?

The moon, Dazzle realized slowly. I'm looking at the goddamn moon.

Wow.

"**Hydration relief procedure initiated**," wasped an emotionless techno-voice, like the robot of Dazzle's dream. "**Please confirm**."

"Hey," Dazzle said, as distinctly as he could through his numb mouth and tingly gums. "All I'm asking for is a little–mmmfff! What the flghhh! Turn it off! You clowns trying to drown me or what?"

The console blinked in self-satisfaction.

"**Subject successfully hydrated. Bowel evacuation mechanisms being activated *now*.**"

Suddenly, Dazzle felt an extremely distressing (and heretofore unknown) sensation occur in his colon, like two plungers coming together. Dazzle just wasn't sure which plunger belonged to the spaceship and which belonged to his bottom.

"*Jeez!*" Dazzle cried. "You guys at Mission Control never warned me about *that*!"

IT WAS GOING to be a long flight, Dazzle thought. So he might as well make the most of it while he could.

He explored classical music, and some of the so-called "world's great books", in the computer's Cultural Database. He learned to type, and eked out a few opening chapters of his autobiography. ("I never asked to be born with a brain–but now that I've got one, nobody's going to goddamn take it away.") He gazed in wonder at the universe emerging all around him–blazing comets and nebulae and galaxies and whatnot. And when he was absolutely starved for company (which wasn't very often) he happily communicated with the shut-down techno-heads back in Houston.

"So I got halfway through a Dostoevsky, and finished a couple Chekhovs," Dazzle told the mouthpiece wired to his forehead. "And frankly, I can't see what everybody gets so worked up about. You'd think if they were truly 'great' artists, they'd paint with a wider brush, and not concern themselves so blind-sidedly with human beings–who, you may have noticed, are pretty uninteresting creatures in the long run. Love, passion, loss, death, ambition–we've heard it all before. Maybe it's Prince Myshkin, or maybe it's some boring guy in "A Boring Story", or maybe it's even some lonely whiz in a Houston control room. But human beings are only a very thin slice of the cosmic pie. Think of all the other creatures out there who deserve to have books and sonnets written about them. Not just dogs, but seals, otters, mongeese, or even alien beings from another planet. How do *they* feel about the perilous state of bio-physiological existence, or the meaningless cosmic thunderbolts that threaten our always-fragile sense of self?"

The best part about annoying the geeks in Houston was that they were locked up in something called Procedural Responsibility. Which meant that they couldn't ignore Dazzle, even when they had absolutely no interest in what he was trying to say.

"**Statement received at Mission Control, Test Subject Doggy. That's a copy.**"

"I'm not looking for you to *copy* me, Mission

Control. Or record what I'm saying for your Mission log. I'm seeking a more direct reply. As in: what do you think about human culture, Mission Control? All these books and symphonies and sonnets and shit. Why doesn't the human race keep all this rubbish to themselves? Why are they so obsessed with launching it into outer space?"

THE MOON LOOMED and diminished. Glimmering, refrigerator-sized asteroids went spinning past; huge astral bodies hove into view and disappeared like semis on the freeway. Jupiter, Saturn, Uranus—and, every so often, a blizzard of unidentifiable particles and ribbony emanations. Dazzle couldn't be sure if it was the universe manufacturing all this beauty, or his own dryly staring eyeballs. It seemed too fantastic and delightfully meaningless to originate anywhere outside his own head.

"Hey there, Daz! I hear you been asking questions that only I, the head honcho on this shindig, can answer. You remember me, don't you, boy? It's your old buddy, Robbie MacShane, chillin' back here in the the good ol' US of A. And by you ess of ay, of course, I mean my ski-cabin in Grasz. You just don't get powder like this anywhere in the world!"

There wasn't a lot Dazzle could say to a guy like Robbie MacShane, a man who had been so successful at everything that he didn't know the meaning of the word irony.

"Always a pleasure, Robbie," Dazzle said, distractedly watching a muted Frasier rerun on the dashboard monitor. That damn Eddie, Dazzle thought. All he cares about's his stupid rubber banana.

"It's fate, Daz. It's Providence and Kismet. The first time I saw your paw-prints on the application form, I shouted, '*What?* Not that holier-than-thou-mutt from the woods again! I thought we were rid of that turkey!' But then it dawned on me. It just seemed so right, like the universe knows how well we work together and wants to bask in our mutual synergy. So are you feeling cozy in your space capsule, pal? You got enough premium Nibbles and lo-cal sodas to keep you satisfied through the Grand Adventure? But even more importantly—are you ready to do business with the greatest unsold demographic in the history of marketing—and I'm talking about the *Goddamn Unknown?*"

It had always been upwards and outwards with R. Wallace MacShane, whose advertising campaign promoting Nibbles Healthy Choice dog food had made Dazzle ("the world's first surgically-adapted talking mutt") a household name from Oak Ridge, Tennessee to Shanghaii and Bombay. ("We veddy much enjoy that talking mutt espousing the health-giving ingredients of Nibbles dog food. It is so veddy American!") Like MacShane's already successful range of sports shoes, frozen vegetarian lasagna, and ergonomically-correct office chairs, Nibbles was manufactured in the poorly accessible mountain villages of Tibet by local school-children and grandparents, then sold throughout the free (and not-so-free) world on the back of a forever-multiplying add campaign (radio, TV, You Tube, and You Name It) that featured MacShane sitting beside a living room fire while his twin daughters knitted sweaters and looked happy, healthy and sensibly-shod. "We all want to do what's right for our dogs, our environment, *and* our families," Robbie explained softly at the end of every endorsement. "But that doesn't mean being healthy has to be boring! Right, boy?" At which point the camera would cut to Dazzle, who looked up from the arts page of his *Wall Street Journal* and added woodenly, with a CGI-smile pasted onto his hairy mug: "Absolutely, Doggy-daddy!"

It had not been the high-water mark of Dazzle's life; but it had paid the bills, and enabled him to open the various 401ks that were now the only thing dividing Daz and his foster-progeny from the pound.

It had also left him with a sense of abiding surrender to the world of market forces over which Robbie presided. So much so that nothing about that world surprised him anymore.

"I guess I've only got one reply to that question, Robbie," Dazzle said, gazing obliquely out at the vast starry night. "Like, have I got a choice?"

"Still the same old Dazzle," Robbie sighed happily. "If there's one thing I've missed about you, it's your goddamn doggish sense of humor. But no, to answer your question—the choices are pretty limited in outer space, bud. Especially when *I* control the food-chute."

AND SO JUST as Dazzle had come to believe that he had escaped the world's smallness, all that smallness had come rushing after him, like one of those interstellar time-vortexes or worm-holes he had heard so much about.

"Testing, testing," Dazzle muttered wearily into the broadcast console as he went rocketing past the constellation Orion. "This is Dazzle the dog communicating on all known wave-bands, please copy. I know you probably don't speak English, being as you're a totally alien species and all–but if you have trouble deciphering this crap? Just let me know and I'll beam you a bunch of Da Vinci drawings, and some egghead mathematical formulas. I missed the meeting, but apparently you're supposed to infer our entire earthly culture from a bunch of logarithms and some stiff lifeless sketches of naked men and women. Go figure."

The universe had never seemed more routine and unsurprising, as if R. Wallace MacShane had shrunk the entire shebang of coruscating nebulae and exploding suns down to his level of comprehension–a slowly scrolling, ticker-tape-like idiot-monitor on the dashboard, which shaped Dazzle's discourse even before Dazzle knew what he was trying to say:

. . . DUMP THE COMEDY, DOG . . . AND READ THE TELE-PROMPTER . . .

"So okay," Dazzle conceded, "this is where I'm supposed to promote today's special offers–and for you Earthlings playing along at home via the continuous web-cam, please keep your guffaws and eye-rolling merriment to yourselves. We'll start with Detroit–yes, we're putting the whole bloody dump on the market, packed to the gills with bankrupt shopping malls and really pathetic sports teams, not to mention fleets of gas-guzzlers and high-quality road hogs. Honestly, these babies can manage maybe five miles to the gallon of icecap-devouring petrol, and feature kid-enslaving back-seat DVD players, surround-sound thunder-boxes, blizzard-generating air-conditioners and bumper-view video cams–you'd be surprised how much meaningless crap you can hammer onto one of these gunboats if you've got government subsidies cushioning your ass. This is a first come, all you can eat, metal-chewer's smorgasbord, so if you're interested, give us a shout and I'll beam you coordinates. What do you say, unseen alien space-types? The ball's in your court, baby. Let's play."

It always left Dazzle feeling slightly grimy and unwashed. Especially when the teleprompter coasted inflectionlessly into its standard sign-off

...END OF COPY...CONFIRM...

and Dazzle heard the food dispenser beep Pavlovianly, extruding a flat orange biscuit that tasted a bit like pasta, but even more like radishes.

And if there was one thing Dazzle hated, it was radishes.

EVEN THE PORTHOLE failed to divulge wonders anymore. There were just more and more uninhabitable planets flitting past, more suns and comets and meteors, and vast dully-glimmering fields of space dust spraying the vacuity in every direction. It was like engaging in a mockery of exploration, Dazzle thought. We aren't out here bravely exploring what we don't know and all that hippie-ish Star Trek rubbish. We're only looking for more of what we already know too well.

"Suckers," Robbie enthused at the start of the next

work-cycle. "If there's one born every minute on our tiny ball of dirt, then just imagine how many are being forged out there in the infinite wonder of space! Billions per nanosecond? Trillions per warp-blink? The endless cosmic frontier promises us a multiple-infinitude of couch-jockeys and midnight web-surfers with nothing on their variously-circuited minds all eternity but what to buy next, and how much they need to borrow in order to purchase some gigantic piece of crap nobody in their right mind really needs. It doesn't take a brainiac scientist to seek out new life forms and alien civilizations, Daz; it just takes perspicacity, and a fervent compulsion to keep earning bucks. I'm telling you, the smartest thing this stupid government ever did was turn the space program over to practical, level-headed space-captains of industry such as myself. At least *I* know what I'm looking for–and not just propelling myself through space on the raw farts of inspiration. So let's get down to brass-tacks, Cosmo-dog. How's the latest radio-survey look? We've been broadcasting on every known wave-band, sixteen hours per day for the past seven weeks. Are we getting any bites? Or should we replot our course for somewhere like, oh, I don't know. Scorpio, or somewhere nutty like that?"

For several days, Dazzle had been drifting in and out of an emerging space-dementia that left him increasingly uncertain about the dividing line between dream and reality. Sometimes, listening to that always-optimistic and enthusiastic voice of American state-sponsored super-corporate capitalism, he thought Robbie was sitting there beside him in the space capsule, miniaturized down to the size and shape of a salted peanut. Other times he looked up and saw the glitchy, sun-lacquered, thickly-happy face of Wally on the console, and thought the salted peanut was speaking to him from Mission Control. In the long run, Dazzle thought, who gives a rat's ass? Reality or illusion—madman entrepreneur or Mr. Peanut sales logo. They're both a big fat con.

"Let me think, Robbie, like how many replies have we received to our broadcasts... let's see... looking over the radio-log here, well, that would add up to *zero*... and as for gross sales, well, that would come to, oh, how do the Mexicans put it, that would come to nada as well... profits, *zilch*; nibbles, *bupkiss*; and as for any cosmic intimations that anybody in your infinite universe wants to purchase oil-drenched Louisiana wetlands, Goldman Sachs certified hedge funds, or a warehouse-full of Neil Diamond commemorative medallions and lead-contaminated baby formula—that all weighs in on the *absolutely not* scale of cosmic consumerism. Let's face it, Robbie. We've finally found a universal demographic that is either so smart—or so entirely non-existent—that it doesn't want to buy any of the crap you're flogging. And I can't say I'm sorry to tell you this, Robbie. I can't say I'm sorry at all."

If Dazzle squinted hard enough, the smiling peanutty face of R. Wallace MacShane squinted right back at him, as if they were locked in some mommy-baby facial exercise. It's getting weird out here, Dazzle thought.

Then the smiling peanut did something Dazzle didn't expect from a peanut—especially one facing a sales-marketing fiasco on the magnitude of this one.

The peanut laughed.

"You just don't get it, do you, dog? When you

believe in the always-expanding, endlessly profitable future like I do, all you need is a set of wheels to take you there. We'll bring home the bacon, Cosmo-dog, one way or another. Just you wait and see."

"I GOTTA BE honest," Dazzle confessed a few work-cycles later, shortly after broadcasting a not-very-heart-felt two-for-one promotional offer on mercury-poisoned frozen tuna and a fleet of last year's Humvee sport-vans, "I never thought my life would turn out like this, flashing through space in a rattly tin can, and trying to sell metaphorical ice to non-existent Eskimos. Even as a pup, I was never an idealistic, Westward-Ho! sort of dog. In fact, I was scared of everything—sheets hanging on a line, my own shadow, the howling of nameless coyotes in the night. If you'd known me then, you'd have been surprised to find me wandering on the street without a collar, let alone going boldly forth into all that Chaos and Old Night. I actually *preferred* sleeping in the basement. I couldn't imagine being anywhere else."

The console-silence that replied to Dazzle's lonely monologue was almost soothing. You can only journey so far into the Unknown, Dazzle thought, until you run out of rope. It's the lesson we all learn eventually. How to go away and not come back again.

"So now," Dazzle concluded, his eyes catching a glimmer of the rousing teleprompter (**PREPARE FOR SECOND-CYCLE BROADCAST TO COMMENCE IN TWENTY SECONDS... NINETEEN SECONDS... EIGHTEEN...**) "I'm suddenly a commercial product spokesperson who's turning the world he loves into something so worthless that nobody in the entire universe wants to buy it, and I guess that makes me sad. Sad to think I've left behind all the things that mattered, and brought with me everything that doesn't. Sad to think I'm exporting commerce to the stars even when you wouldn't catch me dead at a yard sale, let alone roaming through one of those hysterically-decorated mega-malls in Torrance. Sad to realize that maybe there's nothing new to discover on the event-horizon for a washed-out old dog like me. I'm glad Robbie believes in an infinite future—really, I am. But personally, I'm beginning to think us stupid earthlings ran out of future years ago."

It was like being exhausted, Dazzle thought; as if all the word-rich air had expired and left behind nothing but this empty space suit filled with delusions. He had traveled jillions of light years to tell himself the only thing he still cared about and that thing was this:

"I want to go home," he whispered into the console. "I want to see my step-kids and step-grand-kids one more time, and let Edwina take a few more nasty bites out of my ass. Hell, I even want to see Dad, and endure his tireless fuming about the annoying world he can't change. I want to run in the woods I love and never leave them. I want to breathe the clean imperfect air and sniff the dead, mulch-rooted trees and pee in the brush and dig holes in the cakey ground. I'm not ready to go gently into that not-good night. Especially if it means wearing a pasteboard sign advertising federally-disapproved substitute sweeteners, rusting underwater nerve-gas canisters, and underground vaultfuls of decomposing animal-byproducts and human stem-cells. I got nothing to give you, Universe, not even myself. I just want to go home and *be*."

It was a big universe, Dazzle realized sadly. But no longer, he decided, a very surprising one–

...THREE SECONDS... TWO SECONDS... ONE...

–until, that is, the dashboard spluttered with static, and a weirdly unmodulated, explosively-accented voice emerged like the sound of fireworks erupting inside a huge steel shipping container. And what that suddenly surprising voice said was this:

"Hello... *hello*? Are you still there? This is me, a Remotely Accessing Example of Intelligent Life Existing Somewhere Else. I can't quite get the Plumb-plopper working on my Vocal Translation Gland, it's got me sincerely Klittle-stitched, believe me. My name is Glixglax and I come in non-violent appreciation of your selfhood. For several time-units, I've been following your intriguing product-placement assertions, and digesting all these nifty audio books and film-archives you've been so freely distributing–I only hope I can give you something equally valuable in return. So how about we make–what's it called?– 'big wampum' with 'the Great White Father,' if that's okay with you? Gosh, if there's one celluloid-purveyor of fictional truth who rings my Flambles, it's that brilliant Narrative Image-Purveyor you know by the name of John Ford!"

IN THE ANNALS of space exploration, First Contact occurred on a Wednesday, just beyond the third star in Orion's belt, and lasted less than three minutes. But once Glixglax worked out the kinks in his translation-gland, there was no shutting him up.

"On Smurgle," the alien voice fulsomely breathed, betraying a raspy, suboceanic twang in his *t*'s and his *s*'s, "I was never much liked. All the other Smurglians loved each other, but nobody loved me. Every year, at the Divinatory Swirl? I was never invited to commingle. They always made me eat Flurn, while everybody else enjoyed Flurp. Sometimes there'd be this Group Boggle, but nobody ever told me until the next day, and then they always said they forgot, or weren't around, they just made excuses. Stipple them. I made every effort to be liked. I wasn't standoffish. But there was something about me that got up other people's Sturmstubbles. Maybe it's my needy expression, or the way I comb my Dreedles. But whatever the issues dividing me from my species, I'm definitely more a be-on-your own type entity than a group-Boggler. It's just the way I was melded."

Tell me about it, Dazzle thought.

"So that's why I decided to Evacuate my Spore to another Seedling Bed; it took several eons worth of prep. I gathered my Hormonal Supplements in the Reproduction sac, regurgitated profusely, and eventually built up enough Grumpf to make the Big Disconnect. Since then, I've been hiking around the universe on my own, checking out the hot spots for Spore Implantation, and thinking my altogether wooly thoughts of freedom. It's been a perfect choice, self-development-wise. I dig the temperatures out here, all too-icy cold or scalding-hot, no middle ground for me, boy. And I'd almost given up on the idea of other intelligent life forms existing in the universe when I detected your announcement about this great new interstellar commerce idea–and suddenly thought, wow, what a tiny universe. There's original thinkers out here besides me. And the more I thought about it, the more I wanted to get involved. I mean, my race doesn't often evacuate more spores than we can use, but when we do? We're talking a whole Krumload of spores, believe me. I don't know if that phrase translates, but you sound like the sort of entity who gets the picture."

It wasn't the role Dazzle had ever envisioned for himself–acting as intercultural mediator to the stars and all that. He'd actually been crossing his paws for an Empty Universe. The intelligent life-forms he'd *been* dealing with were trouble enough.

"Like, that's cool, Glixglax, but slow down, willya?" Dazzle replied. It was hard to interrupt the alien creature's bubbly overflow of communication; in a way, he was a lot like R. Wallace MacShane. "I'm not trying to prick your bubble, but why don't we take this new cosmic relationship one step at a time and–oh, hold on a second. I've got a memo coming through from the Corporate Chair, so this isn't me talking–it's *him*, and he asks: *Like where's your permanent domicile located? Do you possess any natural fondness for nerve gas or human dung? Have you heard of PayPal? And if so, how soon can we get this shebang on the road?*"

AS IT TURNED out, Glixglax wasn't really an entity. He was more like a space-conglomeroidal conceptual-belief system formed from a self-replicating mass of chaotically differentiated particles and metabolic processes that resembled a coliseum-sized shit-storm. And once he invaded Dazzle's engineering-controls, nobody could tell him to leave. But whatever his

SCOTT BRADFIELD

form, scope or ambition, he was miraculously blessed
with a mega-fast transport drive. Which made
Dazzle's trip home a lot faster than the one going
away.

"Let's face it," Robbie announced at the grand
Welcome to Earth Bazaar that was held on the apron of
the NASA launch site at Cape Canaveral, "nobody
missed that damn dog, but now that he's back, we
don't really mind that he's here!" It wasn't the greatest
welcome-home speech Dazzle might have imagined
for himself, but it was probably the best he could
hope for. "Especially since his outer-space sojourn
has helped us make contact with our greatest, bestest
buddy and favorite intergalactic trading partner of all
time, Glixglax!"

Sometimes, Glixglax's central modulating structure
wavered in places, causing him to resemble a
whirlpool of sentient toasters morphing into a flash
of barbecue grills and back again. It was an
extraterrestrial gesture that Dazzle had learned to
interpret as a smile.

"And Glixglax, as we all know, is pure gold in the
trading partner category, especially since *I'm* gonna
make a bundle knowing him. Now—sorry, Daz, maybe
you could move along, buddy, you're shedding all
over this nice red carpet we've got—perhaps it's time
to load Glixglax up with his various hard-bought
goods and bid him a fond adieu. The sooner he takes
off, the sooner he'll be back. And Glixglax, let me tell
you as a friend and business associate—you will always
be a sight for sore eyes on this planet. Bring your
family! Bring your friends! And hurry back soon!"

Representatives from many recently disgraced
banking and manufacturing conglomerates were all

170

there to claim their piece of the pie. There was a guy from General Motors, and two guys from Citibank, and several more from BP. There were guys from various international stock markets, and a guy from Lockheed, and another couple of weirdly-familiar guys from Halliburton and Blackwater. They were all wearing nice suits and nice shoes, and polite enough to turn off their cells (or at least switch them to vibrate) while the ceremony was in progress.

"So are you hungry, big guy? Are you ready to chow down on all this Earthly splendor?"

There was something about Glixglax you couldn't help but like, Dazzle thought, slinking quietly down the stairs and through the well-trousered legs of America's most unsuccessful (and best paid) capitalists. He's happy with what the universe gives him because he can't imagine anything better.

"Absolutely!" roared Glixglax, in a voice that reverberated throughout the ionosphere. "And then I can give you all something in return!"

At which point, Glixglax relieved himself profusely of his excess metabolic detritus.

And a heap of huge sparkling rocks landed on the red carpet with a beautiful clatter.

"I understand you guys refer to my particular form of waste-evacuants as diamonds!" Glixglax trilled proudly.

It's amazing, Dazzle thought. How things always seem to work out for guys like R. Wallace Macshane.

"*Almost* like diamonds!" Robbie chimed in from the podium, waving his arms in the air as if he had just won a landslide re-election for President. "Only *better!*"

DAZZLE FOLLOWED AN old trail westward that had been favored by pioneers, buffalo, and even two cool dudes in a red convertible, who had starred in a favorite TV show of Dazzle's puppyhood, *Route 66*. It would take a few weeks, he surmised, but he didn't care. The trip home was always the one trip worth making.

The world seemed bigger, drier, and dustier than when Dazzle went away; but maybe that was just west Texas. Or maybe, Dazzle thought, it's me, and the way I see things now. Smaller, less meaningful, simpler, and more fragile—a tumbling ball of gas and rock and liquid hurtling through space. It was funny how things happened. When you went away and came back again it wasn't like you changed. It was more like everything else did.

In historic terms, it was surprising how quickly everybody forgot about First Contact—especially once the docudramas faded into endless repeats on Cable. They forgot about Glixglax, who absconded with his shabby, joyous crap and left behind a suspiciously-shaped heap of diamonds on the Cape Canaveral tarmac which, after it was divvied up by the government and its corporate co-sponsors, was completely forgotten as well. Intergalactic space travel was forgotten, Robbie was forgotten (especially after his sudden fling, remarriage and divorce with a Hungarian supermodel who took him for everything he owned), and even Mission Control was forgotten, fading away into the white-shirt and blue-tied number-crunching whirl of bad haircuts and too-thin ties of NASA, which was soon a wholly-owned subsidiary of the banking, investment and pharmaceutical industries. Good riddance, Dazzle thought.

Less surprisingly, the world even forgot about Dazzle and his weirdly joyous desire for that little bit of out-yonder. And every night, when the stars emerged, Dazzle gazed at them with his old wonder, as if they were places he'd never been. It wasn't what you did or learned or were that made you happy in life, he decided, curling up beside the campfire in his very terrestrial canine compound in Big Sur. It's just knowing that something's out there that you never will do, or know, or be.

Until, of course, tomorrow.

ABOUT THE AUTHOR

Scott Bradfield is a novelist, short story writer, teacher and critic who has long felt an affinity with any animal who doesn't deliberately and willfully contribute to the destruction of its own planet. He lives in London and San Luis Obispo.

Made in the USA
Charleston, SC
13 January 2017